THE
MOUNTAIN VALLEY
WAR

THE
MOUNTAIN VALLEY
WAR

LOUIS L'AMOUR

BANTAM BOOKS
NEW YORK · TORONTO · LONDON · SYDNEY · AUCKLAND

THE MOUNTAIN VALLEY WAR
A Bantam Book / May 1978
The Louis L'Amour Collection / January 1986

If you would be interested in receiving bookends for The Louis L'Amour
Collection, please write to this address for information.

The Louis L'Amour Collection
Bantam Books
P.O. Box 956
Hicksville, NY 11802

ISBN 0-553-06283-2

Published simultaneously in the United States and Canada

Bantam Books are published by Bantam Books, a division of Bantam
Doubleday Dell Publishing Group, Inc. Its trademark, consisting of the
words "Bantam Books" and the portrayal of a rooster, is Registered in U.S.
Patent and Trademark Office and in other countries. Marca Registrada.
Bantam Books, 666 Fifth Avenue, New York, New York 10103.

PRINTED IN THE UNITED STATES OF AMERICA

0   9   8   7   6   5   4   3   2

THE
MOUNTAIN VALLEY
WAR

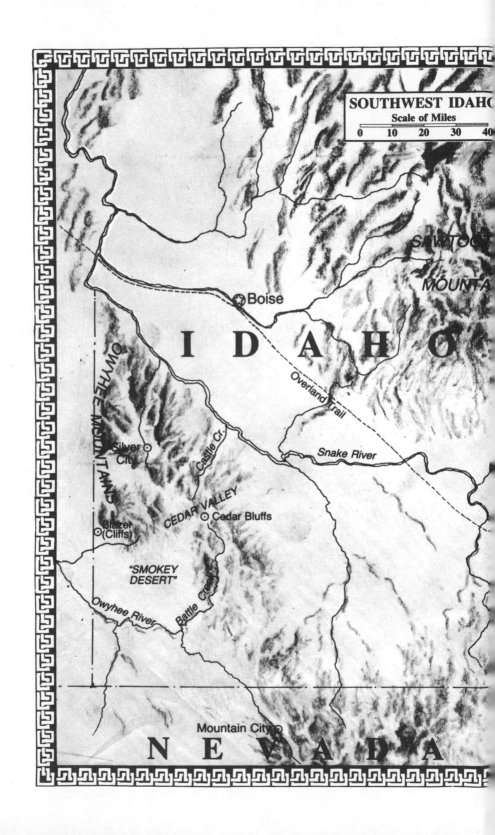

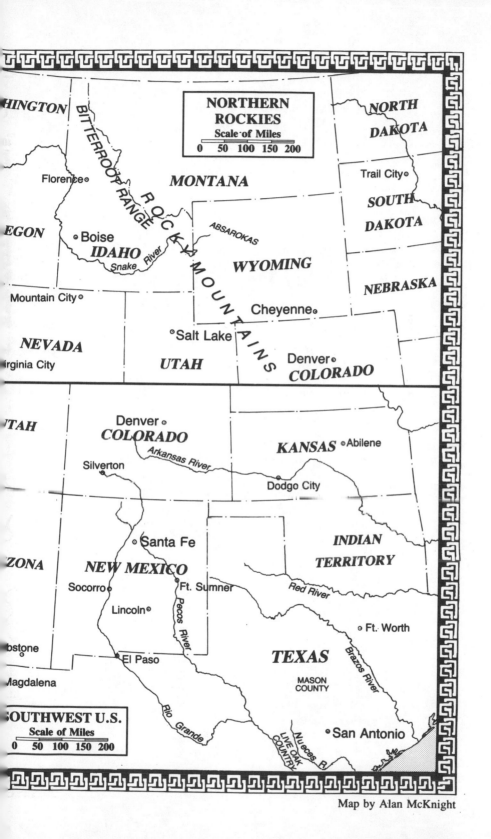

Map by Alan McKnight

ONE

Smoke lifted from the charred timbers where once the house had stood, and curled wistfully in memory of the great barn Moffit had built to store hay and grain against the coming winters. The corral bars were down and the saddle stock had been run off. Where Dick Moffit's homestead had been that morning there was now only desolation, emptiness, and death.

Dick Moffit lay sprawled on the hard-packed earth of his barnyard, the earth deeply clawed in the agony of death. Even from where he sat on the long-legged buckskin, the man known as Trent could see Moffit had been shot at least six times. Three bullets had gone in from the front, the other three fired directly into his back by a man who stood over him. And Dick Moffit had been unarmed.

The small green valley lay still in the lazy afternoon sun, a faint heat emanating from the burned timbers.

So this was the way a dream ended! Dick Moffit had sold a good business back east to try his luck at stock-raising in the far west, something for which he had longed since boyhood.

The man who called himself Trent walked his horse slowly around the burned-out farm. Four or five men had come here, one of them riding a horse with a split right-rear hoof. They had shot Moffit down, then burned his layout.

Yet, where were his children? What about Sally Crane, who was sixteen? And young Jack Moffit, who was but fourteen? There was no evidence of them here, and although the killers might have taken Sally away, they would undoubtedly have killed Jack.

There were no other bodies, nor were there any recent tracks of the children. Those that remained and could be distinguished at all were several days old.

Thoughtfully Trent turned away. The buckskin knew the way they turned was toward home and quickened his pace. There

1

were five miles to go, five miles of rugged trails through mountains and heavy timber and with no clear trail. For this was the way of the man called Trent, that he leave no definite trail wherever he went, and each time he came or went from his mountain hideaway he used a different route, so far as was possible.

He did not expect to be trailed by anyone at this time, but then, many a good man was now dead who had not expected to be followed.

This could be it. Always, of course, he had known the day would come, for trouble had a way of seeking him out, try as he would to avoid it. For too many months now everything had gone too well. The rains had come when needed, the grass had grown tall, his few cattle were growing fat. When in town, he had completed his business and bought his supplies, then returned home. Of course, there had been rumors that King Bill Hale climbed the high meadows, and there was surprise that he had not moved to drive them out.

Slightly more than a year ago he had moved into this high green valley and built his cabin. He found no cattle ranging there, nor signs of them, nor were there sheep. It was a high, lonely place, and the places the others had chosen were much the same, although lower down than his own place. No drifting cowpunchers came this high, and only rarely a lion or bear hunter. His only neighbors were other nesters like himself—Moffit, the Hatfields, O'Hara, Smithers, and a scattering of others.

In the vicinity of Cedar Bluff there was but one ranch. One, and only one. On that ranch and in the town, one man ruled supreme. He rode with majesty, and when he walked, he strode with the step of kings. He never went out unattended, and he permitted no man to address him unless he chose to speak first. He issued orders and bestowed favors like an eastern potentate, and if there were those who chose to dispute his authority, he crushed them without hesitation. With some the pressure of his disfavor was enough. With others he simply offered them a price and their choice was simple: sell out or be forced out.

King Bill Hale had come west as a boy, and even then he was possessed of capital. In Texas he bought cattle, hired the best available men, and drove his herd to Kansas, where he sold at a handsome profit. He learned to fight and to use a gun, and that often a man had to fight to hold what was his. He learned to drive a bargain that was tight and cruel, and to despise weakness. He saw the strong survive and the weak fail, and he determined then to be not only strong but strongest.

He had come to Cedar Bluff, which was on the ragged edge of nowhere, and he drove off those who peddled whiskey to the Indians and the cattle rustlers who used it as a hideout. He drove off the few Indians in the area, and when one honest rancher refused to sell, Hale promptly reduced his offer to half, then bought the one supply store and refused credit. When that was not sufficient, he refused to do business with the rancher under any conditions.

Cedar Bluff and Cedar Valley lived under the eye of King Bill Hale, a strong man and an able one. His ranch prospered, his trading post did well, and he built the Cedar Hotel, a gambling house and saloon he called the Mecca, and then he started a stage line.

He owned sixty thousand acres of good grazing land, which he had bought for prices ranging from a few cents to a dollar an acre. He controlled, by virtue of holding all accessible water, at least a hundred thousand more acres.

He had, aside from enough inherited money to begin at the top, almost unbelievable luck. Of the three trail drives he made to Kansas, not one stampeded, the weather was always good, and the Indians far away. King Bill Hale, however, did not believe in good fortune and was sure he possessed some inherent quality that accounted for his success.

He had been astute, but so had others. He had come along at a time when the cattle business was booming and even some stupid men were making money as a result. He bought beef cattle in Texas for three or four dollars a head and sold them in Kansas for twenty-eight to thirty-five dollars.

In a chancy business where stampedes could scatter cattle all over the range, and where lack of good grazing and water could turn them to little more than hide and hair, he had experienced only success. Now that he was surrounded by those whose success depended upon him, he was free with his money and favors granted, and harsh to all who were not subservient.

He thought of himself as a good man and would have been shocked at the implication of anything otherwise. Those not as successful as himself were "saddle tramps," "nesters," or those who worked for him, who were tolerated if not praised.

Whenever he rode out, he had tough, hard-scaled Pete

Shaw, an excellent cattleman who rode for the brand, and his son, "Cub" Hale.

Behind them trailed the so-called Gold Dust Twins, Dunn and Ravitz, gunmen.

The man who called himself Trent rarely visited Cedar Bluff. The supplies he required were few, the two packhorses more than adequate to carry all he needed for three or four months, and he knew that sooner or later there would be someone from the outside who would say, "That's Kilkenny!"

Men would turn to look, for the stories of the strange, drifting gunfighter were many, although few men lived who could describe him or knew the way he lived. He had no desire for notoriety, no need to be known as a gunfighter, and that he had become so was through no choice of his own but rather a simple combination of traits such as a natural skill with weapons, a cool head and steady hand, as well as remarkable coordination and the experience of years in judging both men and situations.

Mysterious, solitary, and shadowy, he had literally been everywhere. He drifted in and out of cow camps and mining towns, usually unknown, and often a subject of discussion around campfires where he was himself present. Occasionally the moment would come when for one reason or another he must draw a gun, and then for one brief and bloody moment Kilkenny stood revealed for who he was and what he was.

His activities had been many and varied, but no more so than those of many another man of his time and situation, for most men did what was necessary at the time and most were skilled at a variety of trades. He had been a trapper and a buffalo hunter, an officer in the Union Army during the Civil War, a stage driver, a shotgun guard on stages, a cowhand, foreman on a cattle ranch, a tie cutter, a track layer, and a variety of other things. Once involved in a shooting, he never remained in the area, but was gone within the hour if his presence was not demanded at an inquest, and such affairs were few.

In Cedar Bluff he used the name of Trent, and in the high peaks he had found the lush green valley where he built a cabin, ran a few head of cattle driven in from Oregon, and broke wild horses that roamed the utterly wild country to the westward. It was a lonely place, so when he arrived he hung his gun belts on a peg in the cabin and from that time on carried only his rifle.

When in Cedar Bluff, he went only to the general store and occasionally to a small boardinghouse where meals were served, avoiding the Mecca. Most of all he avoided the Crystal Palace, the new gambling house and saloon owned by Nita Riordan.

The cabin in the pines was touched with the red glow of a setting sun when he stepped down from the buckskin and slapped the horse cheerfully on the shoulder.

"Home again, Buck! Feels good, doesn't it?"

He stripped the gear from the horse and turned him into the corral, then carried saddle and bridle into the log barn. He forked hay to the horse, and the marmot in the pile of rocks near the entrance to the trail chewed on some tidbit and paid him no attention. After the first few weeks the marmot had ceased to whistle his warning when Trent approached, no longer considering him a potential danger but rather as part of the normal activity on the mountain. Occasionally Trent placed bits of bread or fruit on the rocks and the marmot ate them, obviously accepting them as tribute from this more or less silent invader.

It was a lonely life with which Trent was content, although from time to time he found himself thinking of the girl in Cedar Bluff.

Did she know he was here? Remembering her from the Live Oak country of Texas where they had first met, he decided that she did, for Nita Riordan had her own ways of knowing all that went on. He did not allow himself to think that she had come here because of him, yet it could scarcely be coincidence that she would arrive in this rather lonely part of the country shortly after his own arrival.

She knew how he felt.

As he went about the business of preparing a meal, he thought of Parson Hatfield and his tall sons. What would the old mountaineer do now? Moffit had been their very good friend, and each had helped the other build when they first filed on land in the mountains. They were hard-working people, intensely loyal to each other and to their friends. Above all, they had a very strong sense of what was right and wrong. If King Bill Hale tried to drive them out, they would fight.

They were the type. They were men who had always worked with their hands, and were beholden to no man. Not one of them was a gunfighter, but each had used a rifle or a short gun all his life and would have been lost without one or the other.

Big Dan O'Hara was another one. A big, bluff Irishman who

had been a track worker, a policeman, and a railroad man back east, always acting as though campaigning for public office. He would fight, of course. No one knowing Dan could believe otherwise.

Hale had shown no interest in the high country until the settlers had moved in. Once it was occupied, it immediately seemed to become valuable to him, or at least to Cub Hale. The fact was that in this country, cut off as it was from other settlements, King Bill wished to be ruler of all that lay about him.

Without doubt war was coming to the high peaks, and the man called Trent thought bitterly of all that would entail. He could not walk out and leave all he had here, any more than he could abandon his friends in their hour of need. Like himself, the others had come to build homes. One and all they meant to remain where they were, each knowing he was unlikely to find anything so lovely again, or with so many possibilities.

There were other things that must be kept in mind. The last time he had visited Cedar Bluff there had been a letter for him from Ranger Lee Hall.

We're getting along all right here, but I thought you should know: Cain Brockman is out and swears he will hunt you down and kill you for killing his brother and whipping him with your fists. And you can be sure he'll try. Be careful.

He dropped four slices of bacon into the pan, humming softly to himself. Then he put on some coffee water and sliced a couple of pieces of bread. He was putting the bacon on a tin plate when he heard a muffled sound from the bedroom.

Instantly he was still. A blanket hung over the door into the bedroom, and his guns hung on a peg across the room. His rifle was nearer.

He went about the business of preparing his meal until close to the rifle, then dropped his hand to it and brought it hip-high. Holding the rifle in his right hand, ready to fire pistol-fashion, he stepped over and jerked back the blanket.

Two youngsters sat on the edge of his bed, a wide-eyed girl of about sixteen and a freckle-faced boy at least two years younger. They stared at him, frightened and pale.

He lowered the muzzle of the gun toward the floor. "How in blazes did you youngsters get *here*?"

The girl stood up and managed a curtsy. Her hair was very beautiful, hanging in two thick blond braids. Her cheap cotton dress was torn and dirty now after the rough treatment of travel.

"I am Sally Crane and this is Jackie Moffit."

"Them Haleses done it! They kilt Pap and burned us out." His features were pale and tense. "I didn't have no gun. I couldn't do anything!"

"I know. I came by that way. You youngsters wash up and we'll have something to eat. Then you can tell me about it."

"They came in about sunup this mornin'," Jack said later. "They tol' Pap he had two hours to git loaded an' git movin'. Pap allowed as how he was on government land, filed on an' settled legal, an' he wasn't movin' for no man."

"And then?" Trent asked.

"The young un, he shot Pap, shot him three times before he could move, then after he fell the young un stood astride Pap's body and emptied the gun into him."

"That, of course, would be Cub Hale." He remembered the slim, pantherlike young man in white buckskins riding his white horse, that handsome young man who liked to destroy anything that thwarted him.

Yet it was not his fight. Not yet it wasn't.

"How'd you kids happen to come here?"

"We had to get away. Sally was gatherin' wood for the fire, just like me, an' when I come up with her, we both started back. Then we heard the talk, and when I started out, Sally, she held me back. I had no gun, and there was nothing I could do but get myself killed, she said."

"Did they look for you?"

"Uh-huh. We heard one of them say he wanted Sally. But they surely couldn't find us, as we knowed that place too well."

"You came here on horseback?"

"Uh-huh. Pap always kept some horses corraled back in a canyon, so we caught us up a couple of them and come over here bareback, ridin' with a mane-holt."

"Pa said," Sally intervened, "that if anything ever happened to him, we were to come to you. You were the closest one, and he said you were a good man and could be trusted."

"Pap said he figured if the truth was known, you were somebody who was almighty good with a gun," Jackie interrupted. "He said you might be on the dodge, but if you were, he'd bet it was nothing you had to be ashamed of!"

"All right," Trent conceded, "you can stay here tonight, and tomorrow I'll ride with you over to the Hatfields'. It's about time the Parson and I had a talk, anyway."

He turned back to the stove. "Looks like I'd best cook up some more grub. I wasn't planning on company."

"Let me do it," Sally suggested. "I can cook."

"She surely can!" Jack said enthusiastically. "She cooked for us all the time."

A horse's hoof clicked on stone, and instantly Trent doused the light. "Down!" he said sharply. "On the floor!"

They could hear the horses coming closer. From the sound, Trent could tell there were at least two and they had split apart to provide less of a target.

"Halloo, the house! Step out here!"

"Who's asking? And what do you want that can't be done better by daylight?"

"It doesn't make a damn bit of difference who it is! We're speakin' for King Bill Hale! You've got until noon tomorrow to get out. You're camping on Hale range!" There was a moment's silence. "We're moving everybody off!"

"Except those you're murdering, is that it?" Trent commented. "You trot right back and tell Hale we're staying. This land was filed on, all fitting and proper, and Hale is bucking the United States government on this, and anybody who helps is a party to it."

He glimpsed the shine of a rifle barrel. "Don't try it, Dunn! If you weren't such a damned fool, you'd know you were outlined against the sky. A blind man could put a hole in you."

Dunn cursed bitterly. "You'll see, Trent! We'll be back!"

"Tell Hale to send me enough men to start a graveyard. And, Dunn, you be sure and come, d' you hear?"

When they had gone, Trent turned to Sally and Jack. "Time for bed. Sally, you take my room, and Jack and me, we'll bed down out here."

"But I don't want to take your bed," she protested.

"Go ahead. You will need all the sleep you can get. This trouble has just started, and it will be a long time before it's over. Get some sleep, now."

"I'm not afraid." Sally looked at him with large, serious eyes. "You'll take care of us, I know."

He stood for a long moment, staring after her. It was a strange feeling to be trusted so implicitly. The childish sincerity of the girl stirred him as nothing ever had. He recognized the feeling for what it was—the need within himself to protect and care for something beyond himself. It was that, in part, that had led him into so many fights that were not his; and yet, was not the cause of human freedom and liberty every man's trust?

There was something else, too, that was not generally recognized—that just as the maternal instinct is the strongest a woman has, just so the instinct to protect is the strongest for a man.

Jack was going about the business of making a bed on the floor as though he had spent his life at it. He was pleased with this chance to show some skill, some ability to accomplish.

Trent checked his guns as he had checked them every night of his life, and for a minute after the checking, he held them, thinking. Then he hung the gun belts on the peg once more.

The time was not yet.

TWO

The early-morning sun was just turning the dew-drenched grass into settings for diamonds when Trent was out of his pallet and roping horses. Yet, early as it was, when he returned to the cabin the fire was lit and Sally was preparing breakfast. She smiled bravely, but he could see she had been crying.

Jack, only now beginning to understand what had happened, was showing his grief through his anger, but was very quiet, moving about the business of taking up the pallets and stowing them away. Trent was less worried about Jack than about Sally, for he knew her story.

According to what Dick Moffit told him, he had found Sally Crane hiding in the bushes some six years before, after he and those with him had come upon a few burned-out wagons. Her family had been murdered by a party of renegades posing as Indians, and she had been picking wildflowers when the attack came, suddenly and without warning.

Dick Moffit and his wife made a home for her, and when Dick's wife had died a year before, Sally had quietly taken over the cooking and housekeeping, which she had only shared before. She had shown herself a cool, competent girl, but two such tragedies were shock enough for anyone to stand.

"You're being a very brave girl, Sally. You'll make some lucky man a good wife."

"I hope to," she said.

"Anybody can take the easy times," he said. "It's when the going gets rough that the quality shows. Now, when we've had breakfast, we're riding over to the Hatfields'. You already know them, so there's nothing I can say except that they are the salt of the earth.

"The Hatfields know who they are, they know what they believe in, and their kind will last. Other kinds of people will come and go. The glib and confident, the whiners and complainers, and the people without loyalty, they will disappear, but the Hatfields will still be here plowing the land, planting crops, doing the hard work of the world because it is here to be done. Consider yourself fortunate to know them."

When breakfast was over he took them to the saddled horses. Then he walked back inside, and when he returned he carried and old Sharps rifle. He held it in his hands for a moment, looking at it, then he held it up to Jack.

"Jack," Trent said, "when I was fourteen I was a man. Had to be. Well, it looks like your father dying has made you a man, too.

"I'm giving you this Sharps. She's an old gun but she shoots straight. I'm not giving this gun to a boy, but to a man, and a man doesn't ever use a gun unless he has to. He never wastes lead shooting carelessly. He shoots only when he has to and when he can see what it is he's shootin' at.

"This gun is a present with no strings attached except that any man who takes up a gun accepts responsibility for what he does with it. Use it to hunt game, for target practice, or in defense of your home or those you love.

"Keep it loaded always. A gun's no good to a man when it's empty, and if it is settin' around, people aren't liable to handle it carelessly. They'll say, 'That's Jack Moffit's gun and it is always loaded.' It is the guns people think are empty that cause accidents."

"Gosh!" Jack stared at the Sharps. "That's a weapon, man!" He looked at Trent with tears of gratitude in his eyes. "I sure do promise, Mr. Trent! I'll never use a gun unless I have to."

Trent swung into the saddle and led the way into a narrow game trail through the forest. He was under no illusions as to what lay ahead. In this remote corner of southwestern Idaho the law was far away and Hale was a widely known and respected man. The natural assumption of any law officers would be that Hale was in the right. He was known as a respectable, law-abiding citizen always prepared to help with any good cause. Those opposed to him would have to prove their case.

"You know, Jack," he commented, "there's a clause in the Constitution that says the right of an American to keep and bear arms shall not be abridged. The men who put that clause there had just completed a war that they won simply because seven out of every ten Americans had their own rifles and knew how to use them. They wanted a man to always be armed to defend his home or his country.

"Right now there's a man in this area who is trying to take away the liberty and freedom from some men. When a man starts that, and when there is no law to help, a man has to fight. I've killed men, Jack, and it's a bad thing, but I never killed a man unless he forced me into a corner where it was me or him.

"This country is big enough for all of us, but some men become greedy for money or power and come to believe that because they have the money and the power, whatever they do is right. Your father died in a war for freedom just as much as if he was killed on a battlefield.

"Whenever a brave man dies for what he believes, he wins more than he loses. Maybe not for him but for men like him who wish to live honestly and decently.

"Hale showed no interest in this land until we moved in here. He's got plenty of land, and every man jack of us filed on our land and we have all built cabins and put in crops. Our part of the bargain with the government has been fulfilled so far, and we have legal right to our land, and Hale has no claim on it except that he wants it. He's never run stock up here and he has never used any water here."

The trail narrowed and grew rough, and there was no chance for conversation. Trent felt the quick excitement he always felt when riding up to this place. It was a windy plateau among the tall pines, and when they topped out he drew rein as he always did at that point to look out over the vast sweep of country that lay below and around.

On one side lay the vast sweep of country in which Cedar Valley was a mere fleck on the great page of the country. A blue haze seemed always to hang over that distant range and those that succeeded it. Here the air was fresh and clear with all the crispness of the high peaks and a sense of limitless distance.

Skirting the rim, Trent led on and finally came to the second place where he always stopped. Westward and south lay an enormous sweep of country that was totally uninhabited so far as anyone knew. Avoided even by the Indians, it was in part a desert, in a greater part merely a wilderness of rocks and lava. Gouged out and channeled by no man knew what forces, there were the beds of long-vanished rivers, craters, weird formations of rock, and canyons impossibly deep and not even to be seen until one reached the very rim. There were places where a reasonably strong man could pitch a rock across a canyon that was two thousand feet deep. It was a vast, unbelievable wilderness, ventured into by no man.

An Indian had once told Trent that his father knew of a way across the country, and even of a horse trail to the bottom of the deepest canyon, but no living man knew it, but nobody seemed to care. It was to most men simply a place to be avoided, but Trent felt drawn to it, his own loneliness challenged by that vaster loneliness below.

Often there was a haze of dust or distance hanging over the area so its details could not be clearly seen, yet Trent had taken the time to ride often to this place and study the terrain below in all its various lights and shadings, for no land looks the same at sunrise as at sunset, and during the day it presented many aspects.

Far and away were ragged red mountains, broken like the stumps of broken teeth gnawing at the sky.

"Someday," he told himself, "I'm going down there and look around, although it looks like the hot mouth of hell."

Parson Hatfield and his four tall sons were all in sight when the three rode into the yard. All were carrying their long Kentucky rifles.

" 'Light, Trent. I was expectin' almost anybody else. There's been some ructions down the valley."

"They killed Moffit. You know Sally and Jack. I figured you could make a place for 'em. Kind of awkward for me, with no woman around."

"You thought right, son. The good Lord takes care of his own, but we uns has to help now and again. There's always room for one more under a Hatfield roof."

Quincey Hatfield, the oldest of the boys, joined them. "Pa tell you about ol' Leathers?"

"Leathers?" Trent's awareness of Hale's strength warned him of what was to come. "What about him?"

"He won't sell nothin' to we uns no more." Quincey spat and shifted his rifle. "That means we got to go three days across country to get supplies, an' no tellin' what he'll do whilst we're gone."

Trent nodded. "Looks like he plans to freeze us out or kill us off. What are you folks planning to do?"

Parson Hatfield shook his head. "Nothin' so far. We sort of figured we might get together with the rest of the nesters and work out some sort of a proposition. I'll send one of the boys

down to round up Smithers, O'Hara, an' young Bartram. Whatever we do, we should ought to do it together."

He rubbed his grizzled jaw and a sly look came into his blue
eyes. "Y' know, Trent, I always had me an idea you was some
shakes of a fightin' man your ownself. I got an idea with some
guns on you'd stack up right with some of those hard cases
Hale has ridin' for him."

Trent smiled. "Parson, I'm a peace-lovin' man who come into
the hills because they were restful. All I want is to be let
alone."

"What if they don't let you alone?" Parson chewed his tobacco slowly, contemplatively.

"If they start bothering me and killing my friends, I might
get upset. You folks want to farm and raise stock. I want to do
that, too, but I also want to sit quiet sometimes and watch the
smoke curl up from my chimney."

Hatfield shrugged a thin shoulder. "I got no worries about
you, Trent. I haven't spent my life a-feudin' and a-fightin'
without knowin' how a man shapes up.

"O'Hara will fight, and so will young Bartram. As to Smithers,
he's a nervy enough man, but he's never had to use a gun.
He'll stand pat, but whether he can make do when it comes to
a downright shootin' fight, I ain't so sure.

"My young uns, they cut their teeth on a rifle stock, so I
reckon when the fightin' starts, I'll be bloodin' the two young
uns like I done the olders back in Kansas."

"What about the women?" Trent asked. "Maybe we should
get them off to somewhere across the wild country before the
shootin' starts. There aren't many of us, and Hale must have
fifty riders, all told."

"He's got the riders," Parson Hatfield admitted grimly. "He
surely has. But I'd ruther tackle the whole fifty than Ma if I
told her she'd have to git out until the fightin's past.

"You got no women of your own, Trent, so you don't know
how impossible ornery one can be when you tell her she's got
to leave, for whatever reason.

"Ma loaded rifles for me when we was feudin' back in Kaintuck,
and she done the same in Kansas when we fit Injuns. She ain't
no ways gun-shy, and when it comes to that, Ma has done a
sight o' shootin' her ownself.

"Quince's wife feels the same, an' so does Jesse's. Those gals
was brung up on the frontier, Trent, and they can stand with a
man whether it be shootin', fightin', or workin'."

Trent shrugged. "You know them better than I do, Parson, but we've got an argument when the others get here. If each one of us tries to guard his own place, we'll be wiped out. It will be one man against a dozen or two dozen or whatever Hale makes up his mind to send. They've got to leave their places and come here, and together we can make a stiff fight of it. Scattered, they'll cut us down one by one."

He turned to his horse. "Parson, I'm going down to Cedar to have a talk with Leathers. We've got to know where he stands, and if he isn't going to sell to us, we have to find another way."

Parson's lean face was bleak. "Reckon they got us by the short hairs, Trent. If we can't get grub, we can't stay on, and whilst huntin' will do some of it, we'd have to have more than we could scratch up."

Trent lifted a hand and turned his horse into a trail. Not the usual trail, for that would be watched, but an old Indian trail known to few. He realized what a chance he was taking, for the killing had begun. Dick Moffit was dead, and he himself had been threatened. Hale riders would be carrying fire and death throughout the mountains now; yet, if he could see King Bill, there might be a chance to avert disaster. There was a chance that Hale himself did not even know of the killing; and if approached, he might stop it before it went further.

Parson Hatfield watched him ride away, then spat into the dust. "Quince, you an' Jesse catch up your hosses and ride along after him. He's surely goin' to git hisself into trouble."

A few minutes later the two tall mountain men had started down the trail on their flea-bitten mustangs. They were solemn, slow-talking young men who chewed tobacco and lived for their crops and their families.

"Quince? What's Pap sendin' us along for? You know that man ain' about to need no he'p."

"He's but one, an' they are many. Maybe Pappy figgers we'll learn somethin'. Anyway, when Trent comes out of Cedar, he'll most likely come a-flyin'. Do no harm to have a couple of rifles to keep folks from crowdin' him too much."

"Well, I got me powder an' shot enough. I'd surely hate to run short when somebody was just a-sweatin' to get hisself shot."

It was going to be one of those white-moon nights when the trees stood black against the sky and there was darkness in the hollows of the hills.

A good night for coon hunting or feudin', and a good night to be hunting them Haleses.

THREE

With no knowledge of those following, Trent rode rapidly. He knew what lay before him and did not, in all honesty, expect results. King Bill Hale was not likely to listen to a mere nester, to someone he considered far beneath him. If he thought of those people who lived in the high meadows at all, he thought of them with some distaste, as a minor annoyance to be brushed aside.

The Hatfields were simple, hard-working people unlikely to ever attain to wealth or more than a competent security. Simple folk they might be, but not to be taken lightly or ignored. They were God-fearing, stern, and fierce to resent any intrusion on their personal liberty. It was such men as these who had destroyed Major Patrick Ferguson and his command at King's Mountain. Not understanding what manner of men he dealt with, Ferguson had threatened them with fire and hanging, and they had responded by coming down from the mountains with their long Kentucky rifles.

These were the sort of men who had been the backbone of all the early American armies. They were fence-corner soldiers who knew nothing of parades but only that war was a matter of killing and keeping from being killed.

They were like Ethan Allen, Daniel Boone, the Green Mountain boys, Kit Carson, and Jim Bridger. They had learned their fighting by constant frontier warfare, and many of their type, the Hatfields included, carried some Indian blood in their veins and carried it proudly.

They knew nothing of Prussian methods of close-order drill, and did nothing by the numbers. Often they had flat feet, and few of them had all their teeth, but they fought from cover and made every shot count, so they lived, while many of the enemy died.

The Hale ranch was the greatest power in this part of the

country, and its riders were hired as much for their ability with guns as for their skill with cattle. King Bill, shrewd as he was, had grown overconfident as he grew older. He had never known men of the Hatfield caliber. His life had been one of continual success, and he could not envision defeat by what he considered a bunch of poor white trash.

Trent considered the question as he rode. Hale might win, but not without a terrible price.

O'Hara? The big Irishman was affable and friendly, yet his easy manner masked a man who was blunt and hard. He wanted no trouble, but his past had been filled with it, from his first arrival from the old country to his years of laying track for the Union Pacific. He had won because he knew not the meaning of defeat. He won because he kept bulling on ahead, blind to the forces against him, blind to all those who opposed him.

As for himself, Trent had no illusions. A peace-loving man he was, yet there was something in him, too, of the old Viking berserk. His good sense told him there was no profit in fighting, but there was a savage something in him that gloried in battle. There was also a fierce resentment for those who abused their power, and a strong streak of rebellion ever ready to well up and express itself in battle.

He had never sought a battle, yet in all honesty he admitted he had never edged too far away from one, either. He now called himself Trent, but the man known as Kilkenny wore the same skin and walked in the same boots.

Had Hale been less blinded by his own success and his power, he would have seen what he was riding into, for Parson Hatfield was no Dick Moffit.

The trail skirted deep canyons, leading down from the high, cool meadows to the hotter flatlands below. At long last King Bill might have realized that when the low country was parched with summer heat the meadows in the mountains lay knee-deep with lush green grass and there were shaded pools and swift-running streams.

On the outskirts of town Trent drew rein to study the situation. Riding in was going to be much easier than getting out. None knew him here, to be awed by his reputation. Anyway, the old days were passing. One heard little of Ben Thompson or King Fisher. Billy the Kid had been killed by Pat Garrett, Virgil Earp had killed Billy Brooks. Names of men once mighty in the west were sliding into the grave or into oblivion.

As for himself, few men could describe him. He had come and gone like a shadow, and where he was now, no man could say, and only one woman.

King Bill Hale owned even the law in Cedar Bluff. He himself had called the election to choose the sheriff and the judge. In the broadest sense, there had been no unfairness in the election. The few nesters and the honest people of the town had too few votes to stand against his fifty riders; and of course, many of the townspeople admired and liked King Bill.

He was always ready to give money to any worthy cause, always superficially friendly. Greeted many people but rarely stopped to talk.

Trent himself had ridden into town to vote, and had voted for O'Hara. There had been no more than a dozen votes cast for the big Irishman. One vote for O'Hara had been that of the one person Trent studiously avoided, the half-Spanish, half-Irish girl Nita Riordan.

She was the only person, so far as he was aware, who knew that he was in fact Lance Kilkenny, the gunfighter from the Texas border country.

Whenever Trent thought of the trouble to come in the Cedar Bluff country, he thought more of Cub Hale than of King Bill. The older man was huge, powerful physically, but not a killer, although he was responsible for the death of more than one person—men he had viewed as malefactors, enemies, trespassers upon land he claimed. But Cub Hale was a killer.

Two days after Trent had first come to Cedar Bluff, he had seen Cub Hale kill a man. He was a drunken miner, a burly, quarrelsome fellow who could have done with a pistol barrel alongside the head, needing nothing more. Cub Hale shot him down ruthlessly, needlessly.

There had been the case of Jack Lindsay, a known gunman, and Cub had killed him in a fair stand-up fight, with an even break all around. Lindsay's gun had scarcely cleared the holster when the three shots hit him. Trent had walked over to the man's body to see for himself, and you could have covered the three holes with a playing card. That was shooting.

There were other stories told of Cub's killings. Two rustlers caught in the act and both killed on the spot. He had killed a Mexican sheepherder in Magdalena for some imagined offense, killed a gunman in Fort Sumner, and gut-shot another in the desert near Socorro, leaving him to die slowly.

Whether Cub was considered or not—and of course, he

must be—there were still Dunn and Ravitz. Both had been involved in a minor way in the Lincoln County War, and both had been in Trail City. Later they left California just ahead of a posse. Theirs were familiar names among the dark brotherhood who lived by the gun, and they were known as strictly cash-and-carry warriors whose guns were for hire.

"Buck," Trent spoke aloud to his horse, "if war starts in this neck of the woods, there will be a lot of killing. I've got to see Hale and talk reason into him."

Cedar Bluff could have been any cowtown. There were three things that set it off: one was the stone stage station, which also housed the offices of the Hale ranch; the others were the two saloon/gambling-halls—the Mecca, owned by King Bill, and the Crystal Palace, owned by Nita Riordan.

It was a time when towns sprang into being overnight, bloomed and boomed briefly, then died. The mines played out or failed to prove themselves, and the prospectors, gamblers, and mining-camp women moved on, following the boom.

There were, as Trent knew from personal experience, several thousand people who followed the booms. Several hundred of them might be found in any new camp. Each dreaming of striking it rich or taking the money from somebody who had, or just following the booms because that was where the excitement was.

Bat Masterson, Wyatt Earp, and dozens like them might be found in Dodge City, Tombstone, Silverton, or anywhere in between. Cedar was off the beaten track, but it was a one-man town, dependent for its existence on the Hale ranch and its hands. There was other trade, but not enough to keep a business open without them.

Trent loped the buckskin down the dusty street and pulled up in front of Leathers' store. He walked into the cool interior. The place smelled of leather and dry goods, and at the rear, where they dispensed foodstuffs and other supplies, he halted.

Bert Leathers looked up from his customer as Trent entered, and Trent saw his face change. Leathers wet his lips and kept his eyes from Trent. Hearing a slight movement, Trent looked around, to see a heavyset cowhand wearing chaps lounging against a rack of saddles. The cowhand took his cigarette from his mouth and looked at Trent with shrewd, careful eyes.

"Need a few items, Leathers," Trent said. "I've a few odds and ends to pick up."

The man Leathers was serving looked up hastily, then averted his eyes. He was a townsman, and at the moment he looked worried.

"Sorry, Trent. I can't help you. You nesters have been ordered off the Hale range. I can't sell you anything."

"Lickin' Hale's boots, are you? I heard it, Leathers, but I didn't believe it. I figured a man with nerve enough to come west and set up for himself would be his own man."

"I am my own man!" Leathers replied sharply, his pride stung. "I just don't want your business."

"When this is all over, Leathers, we will remember that. You're forgetting something, Leathers. This is a country where the people always win in the end. When this is over and we have won, please remember this."

Leathers stared at him angrily; then his eyes fell. His face was white and stiff, and for a moment his eyes wavered to the loafing man near the saddles.

"You all better grab yourself some air," a cool voice suggested.

Trent turned and the gunhand was standing with his thumbs in his belt, half-smiling. "You all better slide, Trent. What the man says is true. King Bill's movin' you folks out, an' I'm here to see Leathers doesn't have any trouble with nesters."

"All right," Trent replied pleasantly. "I'm a quiet man, myself. Rightly I expect I should take that gun away from you and shove it down your throat, but Leathers here is probably gun-shy, and there might be some shootin', so I'll just take a walk."

"My name's Dan Cooper," the gunhand said, "and any time you feel like shovin' this gun down my throat, you just look me up."

Trent smiled. "I'll do that, Cooper, and if you stay with King Bill, I'm afraid you're going to have a lot of lead in your diet. He's cuttin' too wide a swath."

"Uh-huh"—Cooper was cheerful and tough—"but he's got the blade to cut 'em off short."

"Ever see the Hatfields shoot? Take a tip, old son, and when those long Kentucky rifles open up, you be somewhere else."

"You got somethin' there, pardner. You really have. That Parson's got him a cold eye."

Trent turned and started for the street, but Cooper's voice halted him. "Say . . ." Cooper's tone was suddenly curious. "Were you ever in Dodge?"

"Maybe. Maybe I was, Cooper. I've been a lot of places, Cooper, and I've always gone on through and come back.

"Let me add this. I like you, Cooper. I think you've got sand, and I think you're a good man tied in with the wrong crowd. So take a tip from a friendly man. Get on your horse and ride. Make any excuse you can, but ride. King Bill's got the most men, but not the best, and before this is over, a lot of them will be pushing up the daisies. Get on your horse and ride. I always hate to kill a good man."

Trent walked away down the street, and Cooper watched him go, frowning thoughtfully. Where *had* he seen him before? Or had he seen him? Might it be something he'd heard? Some description of a man?

The thought nagged at his consciousness; worst of all, he was apprehensive—and why? Was his memory trying to warn him of something?

He walked back into the store and looked at Leathers. "You got any idea who that was?" he asked.

"He says his name is Trent. He's been around here over a year . . . maybe longer. He's been to town only two or three times. It's almost like he doesn't like towns."

"Or maybe he doesn't like to be where there are people who recognize him. One thing I can tell you, Leathers. That there is a very hard man. See how easylike he handled that? He didn't try to bluff, argue, or throw his weight around, and when a man takes it that calm and easy, it's because he knows what he can do when the chips are down."

Three more attempts to buy supplies convinced Trent he was frozen out in Cedar. Worried now, he started back to his horse. If the nesters could not buy in Cedar, it meant their only recourse was the long, hard trip to Cliffs, or, as some called it, Blazer.

He had grave doubts that even if they started that they would go through unmolested, and their little party was so small they could not spare men to guard the wagons on the long trek over mountains and rugged country.

He tightened his cinch, aware that eyes were upon him and he was about to mount when a voice came from behind him.

"Trent? Nita asked me to ask if you would come to see her." The man was Price Dixon, a dealer from the Crystal Palace, a man who sized up as a straight-shooter.

"All right," he agreed reluctantly, "but it will do her no good to be seen talking to me, or have it known that she talked to me. We nesters aren't looked upon with favor these days."

Dixon nodded. "It looks like you boys are on the short end of it."

"Maybe."

Dixon glanced at him out of the corners of his eyes as they walked along. "Don't you carry a belt gun? They'll kill you someday."

"If you don't pack a gun, you don't have so many fights."

"That wouldn't stop Cub Hale."

"You're right. His sort don't really care whether a man has a chance or not."

Price Dixon studied him thoughtfully as they paused before the Crystal Palace. "Who are you, Trent? What are you?"

"I'm Trent, a mountain-valley nester, what else?"

"Trent, I've been dealing cards west of the Mississippi since the War Between the States ended. I've seen men who were good with guns, and I know the breed. You're not Wes Hardin, whom I knew in Abilene, and you're not Hickok or Masterson or Billy Brooks, you're not Farmer Peel or John Bull, and you never drink much so you can't be Ben Thompson, but whoever you are, you've packed a gun."

"Don't lose sleep over it, Price. A name never made a man. It's always easy to fit a new handle to an old ax."

"You are right, of course, but regardless of the handle, the blade cuts just as deep. No, I won't lose sleep over it, because I'm only standing in the wings, but I have a feeling those who are onstage should be worrying over it. You're a friend of Nita's, and that's enough for me.

"Besides," he added, "Jaime Brigo likes you." He glanced at Trent. "What do you think of him?"

"Brigo?" Trent smiled. "He's part Yaqui, part devil, and all loyal, but I'd sooner tackle three Hales than one Brigo. He's poison."

"I believe you. He sits there by her door day and night, apparently asleep, yet he knows more about what goes on in town than any five other men."

"Dixon? Talk Nita into selling out and getting out. There's a good chance of getting her place shot up or burned out if she stays. This is going to be a long, hard fight."

"Hale doesn't think so."

"Parson Hatfield does. I doubt if Hale has any idea what he's walking into. Nobody has ever bucked him before, and he's bluffing against a pat hand."

"I've seen the Hatfields. I grew up in the South, Trent, and now and again I'd see those men come down from the hills, and I've never forgotten them."

Trent opened the door. "Dixon, stay by her. I am afraid she will need all the friends she's got, once this starts. And try to keep her out of it."

Dixon shrugged and smiled, then shook his head sadly. "I think you've known her longer than I have, Trent, and Nita makes her own decisions, always. Also, she's afraid of nothing."

"Then stay by her. She will need all her friends, and I'll be out there in the mountains."

He went inside, where all was cool and still. Only two men, both strangers, stood drinking at the bar, as the hour was still early. This was suppertime in Cedar.

He looked over his shoulder. The sun was setting and the street and the walls were red—like blood.

FOUR

The Crystal Palace was one of those places that made the West what it was. Wherever money was to be spent there would be found the saloons and gambling houses, yet they were not alone for drinking and gambling, for the western saloon was a meeting place, a political forum, a clearing house for information, a place where business deals were consummated, and a club room as well.

Money was being made in the West, whether in cattle, buffalo hunting or mining, and the men who were making it were, largely speaking, free spenders. They had the money and they wanted the best in rare wines, champagne, excellent food, and elaborate decor.

Cedar had the well-paid cowhands from the Hale ranch, certainly not making big money but better money than others in an equal position. There were miners, also, some from as far away as Florence or Idaho City, for the Palace offered the best.

Nita Riordan, as Trent could see, was doing all right. She had inherited her first gambling house and saloon when she was several years younger, and had inherited Jaime Brigo at the same time.

Young as she was, she was a shrewd businesswoman whose predecessor had taught her the business. There was no necessity for crooked games, and Nita would not permit anything of the kind. The house percentage was sufficient. It also meant less trouble. If any disgruntled loser complained that he was cheated, she immediately repaid the sum he had invested, but he was never permitted inside the doors again. Knowing this, even the poor losers rarely argued, for none wished to be denied the best place in town with undeniably the best food in the territory.

Trent knew a little about gambling houses, and this one obviously was doing well.

Price Dixon led the way across the room. Jaime Brigo was there in a black velvet suit, white shirt, and his two guns. A knife was also at his belt, and Trent remembered that he carried another down the back of his neck, ready for a quick grasp and a throw.

"*Buenos días, señor!*" Brigo flashed his white teeth.

Dixon stopped and gestured to the door beside which Brigo sat: "She is in there."

Trent faced the door, drew a deep breath, and stepped inside. His heart was pounding and his mouth was dry. No woman had ever affected him as this one did, none had ever stirred him so deeply or made him realize how much he was missing in his lonely life.

It was a quiet, pleasant room, utterly different from the garish display of the gambling hall. It was a room to be lived in, the room of one who loved quiet and peace. On a ledge by the window were several potted plants, on the table lay an open book. These things he absorbed rather than observed, for all his attention was upon Nita Riordan.

She stood across the table from him, taller than most women, with a slender yet voluptuous body that made a pulse pound in his throat. She was dressed for the evening, an evening of walking among the gambling tables, and she wore a black and spangled gown utterly out of keeping with the room in which she stood.

Her eyes were wide, both hands held out to him. "Lance! Why have you waited so long?"

"You've not changed," he said. "You are the same."

"I'm older, Lance. More than a year older."

"Has it been but a year? It seems much longer." He looked at her thoughtfully. "You are lovely, as always. I think you could be nothing but lovely and desirable."

"And yet when you could have had me, you rode away. Lance, do you live all alone in that cabin of yours? Is there no one?"

He chuckled. "Nita, if there was anyone you would know it. I think you are aware of all that goes on. Yes, I am alone except for the memories, and they only make it worse. Yet when I think of you and all that could be, I remember Bert Polti, too, and the Brockmans. I wonder how long it will be before I go into the dust myself."

"That's one of the reasons I sent for you." She came around the table and took his hands again. "Lance, you've got to go.

Leave here now! I can hold your place for you, if that's what you want. If that doesn't matter, just say the word and I'll go with you. I will go anywhere with you, but we must leave here *now!*"

"Why?" It was like him to be direct and to the point.

She looked up into his dark, unsmiling face.

"Why, Nita? How do you imagine I could leave the others, who depend upon me? Well, to a degree, at least."

"Because they mean to kill you! Lance, they are cruel and vicious. I am not speaking of King Bill, although he is their leader, for what he does he believes to be right. It's Cub.

"He loves to kill, Lance. Last week he killed a boy in front of my place, then shot into him as he lay on the walk. He's not normal, Lance. He's insane, and not even his father is aware of it.

"When he is with his father, he is always at his most charming, and I believe he truly loves him. King Bill at least uses his power to build, even though he rides roughshod over others in the process. Cub uses power only to destroy."

"I must stay. There are so few of us."

"Lance, I've heard them talking. Oh, they wanted me to hear! They conceal nothing because they believe no one can touch them. Or would wish to touch them.

"They are sure you will fight, so they mean to kill you. Even now they know you are in town, and they do not plan to let you leave. They won't give you a chance."

"Nita, the people in the high meadows are my friends. I cannot be the first to break and run."

"They don't know you are Lance Kilkenny, but they do suspect you are someone whose name is known. I believe they think you are some outlaw on the dodge. They mean to kill you. It is that simple."

"Nita, I have been through this before. Perhaps the odds were less, but the game was the same. No, I must stay."

He paused. "I must talk to Hale. He could stop this if he would. He has to be made to understand."

"There isn't a chance! Not one. He lives in a world all his own. No one even dares address him, and if you approached him he would be offended. You would not have a chance to speak. And don't forget, the man's not over forty and he's a fighter."

"You seem to know him well. Has he made you any trouble?"

"What makes you ask that?"

"I want to know."

She shrugged. "He wants to marry me, Lance." She smiled suddenly. "I will admit that he told me so somewhat in the manner of a king conferring a boon upon some lesser creature, but nonetheless, he did ask."

Trent stared at her. "And you, Nita? What did you say?"

"I am lonely, Lance. I have no life here, only a business. I know no women but those of the dance hall. Oh, they're a pretty good lot, really. And my girls are strictly dancing partners, nothing more. It may be that one or two of them have found friends . . . I wouldn't know about that, and it is their own business, but I know no one else, see no one else. I am dreadfully, frighteningly alone.

"King Bill is strong. He knows how to appeal to a woman. He has a lot to offer, and even though he has a son as old as I, he's still a young man. I do not like what he is doing, but he can offer many arguments why he believes he is right.

"No, I will not marry him. Even if you were not here, I would not. I've been tempted, I will admit, but he's a little insane, I think. He got too much money and too much power and it all came too easily. He believes he is better than other men because he has succeeded. But whatever you do, don't underrate him . . . or Cub."

"You spoke of him as a fighter. You mean he will have his men fight?"

"No. I mean *he* will fight. He told me once in such a flat, ordinary voice that he could kill any man with his bare fists."

"I want no trouble with him. Only a few minutes' conversation."

"Shaw, his foreman, tells a story about King Bill killing a man with his fists in El Paso, and another on the ranch. These were men who challenged him personally."

"I must see him today, Nita. He must be convinced his best recourse is to leave us alone. He doesn't need our land, and none of us are thieves. We encroach upon him in no way."

"He won't talk to you, Lance. I know him. He has made a big thing of not being addressed by anyone to whom he does not speak first. He will just leave you to his bullyboys."

"He'll talk to me."

"Don't go over there, Lance. Please don't."

"Has he made trouble for you?"

"No. So far, he has listened to me and we have talked very

quietly. None of the others have made trouble, either, largely because they know he is interested in me.

"There was an attempt at a holdup one night, but they may not have been his men. At least, nobody ever claimed them."

"What happened?"

"They didn't know about Jaime. I was counting the receipts for the week, when they came in with guns. Jaime had just stepped out for a minute and then he stepped back in. They were facing each other, both with guns in their hands, and one of them said, 'Looks like we tackled more'n we expected. All right if we back out now?' And Jamie said, 'No.'

"They didn't understand. It was a Mexican standoff, and it seemed to them the best thing was just to back out. But you know Jaime, he just said 'No' and they stared at him and one said 'No?' And Jamie shot them both.

"Since then there has been no trouble. But I have no illusions. If King Bill wants this place . . . or me, he will stop at nothing. Or the minute he steps out of the picture, Cub will be there."

"Well"—he turned to go—"I must see him. I've got to make at least one attempt to stop this before it gets started. I can't bring Moffit back, but maybe I can save some others."

"And if you fail . . . ?"

"I'll buckle on my guns and come to town."

He paused in the outer room to watch Price Dixon dealing cards, but his mind was not on the game. He was thinking of King Bill and how to approach him.

Hale fought to win. In this little corner of the West there was no law but that of the gun and what men chose to impose upon themselves. By and large, western pioneers wanted law and order and were law-abiding people, although there were always those who were lacking in self-discipline or were heedless of the rights of others. Hale would have been the last man to flout the law. In fact, he sincerely believed he *was* the law.

There were few trails in or out of the country, and Hale had always been careful to see that no potential troublemakers reached the area, or, if they came, did not long remain. Even what news left the valley depended much upon Hale. The echoes of the trouble to come might never reach beyond these hills.

Hale himself lived in a ranch house two miles from Cedar, a place referred to locally as the "Castle," and rode into town once each day for a brief stop at the Mecca and occasionally at the Crystal Palace. Trent decided the logical place to find him was the Mecca, as he did not wish to bring trouble to Nita by meeting him here.

Trent knew what Nita meant when she spoke of being lonely, for there had been few times in his life when he had not known the feeling. He had been born on the frontier in Dakota, but his father had been killed and he had lived with an uncle in New York and then with an aunt in Virginia. They had been kind, always, but he had been left much alone.

Trent walked out on the dark street. He led the buckskin to water, fed him some hay, then led him back to the hitching rail.

There were few people around, but the sounds of music came from both the Mecca and the Crystal Palace. Dan Cooper had left the store and was sitting on the steps outside. He watched Trent, then strolled over to where he was tying the buckskin.

"If'n I was you, Trent," he said, "I'd fork that horse and light a shuck. You ain't among friends."

"Thanks, Cooper. I take that as a friendly tip, but I've got business. I don't want a war in Cedar, and I want to make one more attempt at stopping it."

"And if you don't?"

"Then I'll have to take steps."

Dan Cooper began to build a cigarette. "You sound all-fired sure of yourself. Who are you? What are you?"

"Like I said, old son, I'm a nester named Trent."

He turned to stroll off down the boardwalk, and as he did so, a small cavalcade of riders rode down the street from the Castle and drew up before the Mecca. Four men, and the big man on the bay would be Hale.

Hale got down and led the way through the batwing doors. Cub followed, while Ravitz tied Hale's horse. Dunn stood for a moment looking toward Trent, whom he could not quite make out in the gloom under the awning. Then he walked inside.

FIVE

Trent pushed open the doors and stepped into the now crowded saloon. Most of those present seemed to be Hale cowhands, but there were a few prospectors and miners coming from or going to the gold camps to the north. At the bar, King Bill was standing, his broad back turned to the room.

He was big. Perhaps an inch shorter than Trent's six feet and one inch, he was much the heavier of the two. He was broad and powerful, with a massive chest, his head a block set upon a muscular neck, his jaw broad and strong. He was a bull, and Trent, looking at him now, could well believe the stories of his killing men with his fists.

Beside him, in beautifully tanned and dressed white buckskin, was Cub Hale, and on the far side of Hale were Dunn and Ravitz.

Trent walked to the bar and ordered a drink. Dunn, hearing his voice, turned his head. As their eyes met, the glass slipped from Dunn's fingers and crashed on the edge of the bar.

"You seem nervous, Dunn," Trent suggested. "Let me buy you a drink."

"I'll be damned if I will!" Dunn said. "What d' you want here?"

Trent smiled. All the room was listening, attracted by the fall of the glass and Dunn's explosive question. Of those present, some would be townspeople who might not have chosen sides.

"Why, I just thought I'd ride down and have a talk with King Bill." He spoke calmly but clearly, so that all might hear. "It seems there has been a lot of war talk, and somebody killed a harmless family man on his own doorstep the other day, killed him when he was unarmed and totally defenseless. It struck me that King Bill would want to know about it."

"Get out!" Dunn ordered, his hand hovering near his gun. "Get out or be carried out!"

"No use to reaching for that gun," Trent replied calmly. "As everybody can see, I am not heeled. And I am here to make peace talk with King Bill."

"I said *get out!*" Dunn replied.

Trent was still smiling when Dunn's hand suddenly dropped for his gun. Instantly Trent moved. His left hand dropped to block the gun hand, the right whipped up in a short, wicked arc and exploded on Dunn's chin.

The punch was short but perfectly timed, and it caught Dunn on the point of the chin. He started to drop, and Trent let go of the gun wrist and let him fall, but as he did so he slipped the gun from Dunn's holster and placed it on the bar.

Trent turned to Hale. "Sir, some of your men invaded our area and murdered Dick Moffit, then burned him out. They ran his young children into the woods, homeless and hungry, then hunted them to try killing them as well. Those same men warned me to move out. Now, I've heard you are a fair man, so I have come to you."

King Bill did not move or give any indication that he heard. He looked at the whiskey in his glass, tasted it, and put it carefully back on the bar.

Cub Hale had moved away from him, poised and eager. "Hale," Trent said, "this is between you and me. Call off your dogs. I am talking to you and nobody else, and what is said here tonight will be repeated up and down the country. We want peace, but if we have to fight to keep our land, we will fight. If we fight, we will win. You are bucking the United States government now, Hale, as all our land has been properly filed on and we are proving up."

Cub was waiting. At a word from his father or even a gesture, he would draw. Trent was unarmed. He felt cold and tight, and knew that never had he been so close to death.

"What's the matter, Hale? Are you going to make a murderer of your son because you're too yellow to talk?"

Hale turned slowly. "Cub, stay out of this. I'll handle it."

Cub hesitated, alive with eagerness and disappointment.

"I said," Hale's tone was harsh, "get back and stay out of this."

He looked at Trent for the first time, his eyes cold and ugly. "As for you, you've squatted on my range. Now you're getting off, all of you. If you don't leave, you'll take what you've got coming, and that's final."

"No, Hale, it is not final. We are filed legally, and we intend to stay. You made no claim on any of that land until we moved on it and started developments. If we don't get justice, we will have a United States marshal in here to find out why."

"Justice! You grangers will get all the justice you need from me! I've given you time to leave. Now, get!"

Trent stood his ground, yet his own anger was welling up within him. The unreasonableness of the man irked him. Ruthless as he might be, he might also be basically a square shooter.

"Hale," he said, "I've heard you're a fighting man. I'm calling you now. We fight, man to man, no holds barred, and if I win, you leave us alone, if you do, we leave."

King Bill turned, his fury swelling the veins in his neck. "*You!* You challenge *me?* You dare? You, a dirty-necked nester, a farmer? No! I bargain with no man. Move out or suffer the consequences."

"What's the matter, Bill! Are you afraid?"

For a long moment there was silence in the room, and then Hale unbuckled his gun belt. "All right, nester, you asked for it."

He swung suddenly, a vicious backhand. Expecting something of the kind, Trent sidestepped easily, and Hale nearly went off balance with his blow.

"What's the matter, Bill? I'm right here."

Hale moved in fast, swinging both fists. Trent met his rush with a left jab that split both his lips and showered him with blood. For an instant the larger man was stopped still by the shock of seeing his own blood. Then in a fury he closed in. Trent evaded the first blow, but a powerful right swing caught him alongside the head, and he staggered back on his heels. His blood staining his gray shirt, Hale closed in fast. He hit Trent again. Trent evaded another punch, more by good luck than skill, and closed with him, smashing away at Hale's body with both fists.

Throwing him off, Hale knocked him to the floor with a left. Trent rolled over and climbed to his feet, but was knocked down a second time, his head roaring with sound. As he rolled over to get up, somebody kicked him viciously in the ribs, and he caught a glimpse of Cub's malicious grin.

Hale rushed, swinging with both fists, but Trent went inside of a left and smashed a right to the heart. Hale grabbed him and threw him against the bar, then charged, swinging hard with both fists, knocking his head from side to side. Desperately Trent lunged to get away from the bar, but Hale pushed him back, measured him with a left, and started the right that was to finish it.

Trent whipped a wicked left to the wind that wrenched an agonized gasp from the bigger man, who missed with the right. Trent stabbed another left to the bleeding mouth, but Hale floored him again with a right. Trent lunged up as another kick was aimed at him. Hurt, gasping with pain, he clinched with Hale and hung on desperately, fighting to clear his head. Hale threw him off and swung a left that cut his cheek to the bone. Trent stabbed the left to the mouth again and followed it with a right to the ribs.

He ducked under a right and smashed Hale in the belly with another right, then hooked a left over Hale's shoulder to cut him over the eye.

Hale rushed at him, grabbing for his throat, and Trent felt himself falling backward. He fell, but as he did so he grasped Hale's upper arms, put a boot toe in his stomach, and as he fell he pitched the larger man over his head to the floor.

King Bill staggered up, visibly shaken. Trent staggered back against the bar, wiping the blood from his eyes with the back of his hand. Hale was hurt, and he was shaken. Perhaps in that moment the bigger man realized for the first time that he might be beaten.

Trent moved in swiftly. He lanced a left to the mouth, crossed a right to the chin, and as Dunn started to come in, Hale waved him back. He put up his hands, his face twisted with hatred and fear. He started forward, and Trent feinted; as the hands moved, he struck hard with his right and Hale staggered and almost fell.

They stood toe-to-toe then, and both began to swing, but the power had gone from Hale's blows. The hard years of work that lay behind Trent now were saving him; he was getting his second wind now, steadying down. His head buzzed with the blows that had left him groggy, but he knew now what he had to do. He feinted again and struck hard with left and right. He feinted again and then threw both fists to the midsection. Hale's knees buckled, and Trent threw hard to the chin. The big man was slammed against the bar by the force of the

punch, and as Trent moved to face him, he caught a glimpse of
Cub.

The younger man's face was twisted with shock and something like horror, but mingled with it was something else, a
kind of evil delight in what was happening. Sickened, Trent
stepped back and moved around.

Hale was game. He started forward, and Trent swung a hard
right to the jaw. The big man started to buckle at the knees,
and Trent hit him before he could fall.

He fell then, flat out on the saloon floor, and he lay still.
Trent, looking down to see if he would try to get up, felt a
pang. It was a hard, hard thing to be so long a winner and then
to be beaten, and beaten thoroughly, and in front of all these
others over whom he had lorded it.

Had he been anywhere but surrounded by enemies, Trent
would have picked the man up and told him he was sorry.

In the moment of silence, a cool voice spoke out clearly.
"Now, you all just hold to w'ar you're standin', because I ain't
a-wantin' to kill nobody, but sure as I'm Quince Hatfield, this
here rifle is aimed an' steady."

Nobody moved or spoke, for the intent of the rifle was plain
enough, and from the door they could see another. How many
more there might be, they did not attempt to guess.

In three steps Trent was across the room and out-of-doors
into the night. The buckskin was waiting for him at the edge of
the boardwalk with the Hatfield horses, and he swung to the
saddle and with almost the same motion slipped his Winchester from the boot. With a quick shot he sent the chandelier
crashing, and then they were gone. A mile out of town they
slowed down and Quince came up alongside.

"I d'clare, Trent, when you all set out to start somethin',
you surely don't fool around! You just busted things wide
open."

Trent shrugged, and it hurt so much that he almost cried
out. Every move he made, he discovered another sore spot. "I
tried to talk peace, but he wouldn't listen. Then I thought a
good licking might teach the townspeople that he wasn't all-
powerful. We're going to need friends."

"The Parson will be some upset when he hears about this,
and him not seein' it. He's said time and again that all Hale
needed was a good whoppin'."

"It will take more than that," Trent said. "He was a tough

man to whip, and when he's able, he'll find another way. He's got the men and the money, Quince. We've only got ourselves."

"Maybe that's all we'll need, that an' the good Lord's help."

Nothing had been solved by the fight, and no allies would have been gained. Still, there might be a few who would now be doubting the outcome.

Taking to the brush, they used every stratagem to ward off pursuit, although it was doubtful if any pursuit would be attempted in the darkness.

Three hours later they pulled up at the Hatfield cabin. A tall young man stepped out of the darkness to greet them.

"It's us, Saul," Jesse said, "an' you missed a scrap! Trent done whupped King Bill Hale with his fists. Whupped him good."

"Reckon Pa will be please' to hear that!" he said. "And I am, m'self. Whupped him, you say? Wow! That must have been some fight!"

"They all abed?"

"Sure. Lijah was on guard up until a few minutes ago, but knowin' him, he's dead to the world by now."

"O'Hara here?" Trent asked. His jaw felt stiff and sore, and he ached in every muscle and bone. Hale was a puncher, and he had landed more often than he missed.

"He's here. Him, Bartram, an' Smithers. Come mornin', Pa wants us all to get together and figure out what it's best to do."

"We will have to fight," Trent said. "There's no question of that now. Hale wouldn't talk peace."

"So you whupped him. Serves him right. Nobody up here wants a fight, but we're all ready for it. We'll do what has to be done."

"I've a blanket and my slicker. I'll bed down over against the brush after I've washed up."

When he had stabled the buckskin, he stripped off his shirt and bathed in the water trough. The water came from a spring in the shoulder of rock and was piped into both the house and the horse trough, where a continual flow kept it fresh.

The cold water felt good on his swollen, battered face. One eye was swollen almost shut, and there was a nasty cut on his cheekbone that might need a couple of stitches. He would see about that in the morning. Ma Hatfield was good at such things, but young Bartram had worked with a doctor for over a year and had planned to practice before deciding to come west.

He carried his blanket and the slicker to a corner of the

woods near the spring and rolled up. Yet it was a long time before he fell asleep. His hands were swollen from the battering they had taken in punching Hale, although he had gone to the body as much as possible.

What would happen in Cedar now? Would the Hales hear of his visit to Nita? Had they any idea the two were old friends? He doubted that, and doubted they would know more than that he had gone to the Crystal Palace, a not unexpected thing, since the Mecca was controlled by Hale.

Slowly, as he lay awake, he turned over the various choices they had. They were outnumbered at least five to one, but that troubled him less than supplies.

There was game in the mountains, but not so much that it would not be seriously depleted by trying to live off it. Each of the families had some stores against bad weather or attack, yet none of them had enough. Supplies of food and ammunition were of first importance, and there was no chance in Cedar. . . . Or maybe there was.

An idea came to him, and he considered it from all angles, and somewhere during his considerations he fell asleep.

When he awakened again he lay for a few minutes watching the first graying of the night come to the Hatfield ranch. Slowly things became distinct. The peeled bars of the corral, and handmade shakes on the barn roof, the carefully hewn timbers of the log house. Parson Hatfield and his sons had expended much hard labor here, but everything was made with a loving touch. They had been building a home, not just a house.

He sat up. If he had his way about it, this would be their home as long as they wished to stay.

SIX

The morning sun had scarcely lifted over the pines when the men gathered around the long table in the Hatfield home. Breakfast was over and the women had gone on to other work.

Trent sat at the foot of the table, making few comments. He was tired and stiff. One eye was black and badly swollen. He had four stitches taken in a cut on his cheekbone, and his lips and one ear were puffed and red. He was in no mood for conversation, yet it had to be. Looking at those around the table, he could not but wonder how many would be present when the time came to celebrate a victory, if there was to be one.

More than any of the others, he knew what lay ahead. The years since boyhood had dealt hardly with him, and on more than one occasion he had seen such troubles start, and so far he had lived to see them end. Many of those with whom he had worked and fought had not survived.

The five Hatfields were there. O'Hara and Bartram. The big Irishman was a game man who among other things had been a policeman in New York. Bartram was young, keen, and a man who had grown up, as most of them had, hunting meat for the table. He was excited by what lay ahead, and was ready for anything and everything.

Smithers was quiet and middle-aged, the oldest of them but for Parson himself. He was a small man, precise in his thinking and planning, avoiding trouble yet seemingly fearless. He was the best farmer of the lot, and the best businessman.

Two more rode in while they were sitting at breakfast. Jackson Hight was a wild-horse hunter, a former cowhand and buffalo hunter, and Steve Runyon a former miner.

Parson Hatfield cleared his throat. "This here meetin' better come to order. Them Haleses ain't about to wait until we uns get organized. There's a few things come first. We got to pick us a leader, and we got to find some way to get grub and ammunition."

Trent spoke up. "Parson? If I can put in a word. I believe it would be safer if we all came here, bringing what supplies and horses we can."

"And leave our places?" Smithers objected. "Why, they'd burn us out! They'd ruin our crops and run off our stock!"

"He's right," O'Hara agreed. "If we aren't there to defend them, they won't last long. That's playing right into their hands."

"Which of you feels qualified to defend himself against twenty gunmen? I don't feel I could. There isn't a place among yours where one man could stand off five men, let alone several times that many. You can only shoot out of one window at a time. They'll get around you, and you'd be dead within minutes.

"There's but two places among us that can be defended with any chance of winning. Mine and the Hatfields', and mine won't handle all the people we've got. Hatfield has more supplies on hand, he's got a place that can be defended, and there's already five men on the spot.

"If we get burned out, we can rebuild. Hell, there isn't a man here who hasn't already built more than once. But if you're dead, you aren't going to build anything."

"Strikes me as sensible," Hight said. "It's the old argument, 'united we stand, divided we fall,' so I move we all come together here."

"You may be right," O'Hara agreed. "Dick Moffit didn't do very well alone."

"That means I'll lose my barn!" Smithers protested.

Nobody said anything, and after a minute he said, "Well, I can always build a new one, even if it takes ten years."

"We will all help," Bartram replied.

"How about a leader?" Smithers asked. "How about you, Parson?"

"No, I'm obliged, but I ain't your man. I move we choose Trent here."

There was a moment of silence, and then O'Hara said, "I'll second that motion. After all, he whipped Hale."

Runyon shook his head. "No offense, Trent, but I don't know you. Fistfighting is one thing, handling a fight like this will be another. I've got no objections to Trent, but after all, Parson, you've done a lot of feudin'."

"That I have," Hatfield replied, "but let me say this here.

Onct I was a sharpshooter and I rode with Jeb Stuart. One time ol' Jeb he sent us off on a special detail, and we'd been sent like that often, because we always got the job done. Well, this last time we got our socks whupped off us by a youngster Union officer. He only had half as many men as us but he surely outmaneuvered us an' whupped us."

He poured coffee around the table, then put the pot down. "Point that I'm makin' is that that young Union officer who whupped us so bad, that was Trent here." He smiled slyly, eyes twinkling. "I never said nothin' to Trent about rememberin' him, because back then he had a different name than now, and a man's name is his own business."

"That's good enough for me," Runyon said. "If you say he's got the savvy, I'll take your word for it."

"All right." Trent wasted no time. "Mount up and go home, bring all you can load easy of ammunition and grub, but get back tonight. Two of you ride together as much as possible, and watch your back trail. They will be coming, you can depend upon it, and I want all of you back here alive. We need every man. . . . Don't try to fight unless you cannot get away, just come on to the Hatfields'."

Trent got to his feet. "We will let Hale make the first move. That isn't tactically sound, but we must have the law on our side. If they attack first, we have every right to defend ourselves.

"When Hale moves, we will move too. We've got twelve men—"

"Twelve?" Smithers looked around. "I count only eleven."

"Jack Moffit's number twelve," Trent replied. "I gave him a Sharps. Jack is fourteen, and at fourteen many of us have done a man's job. I'll stake my saddle that Jack Moffit will do his bit. I've seen him bark squirrels with a good rifle, and a squirrel's not as big as a man."

He paused. "We will have six hold this place, and six can do it. With the other six, or with four or whatever we need, we will strike back, go after grub . . . whatever."

"That's the kind of talk I like," Smithers said. "I've not been a fighting man, but I dislike to think of my property destroyed when they get off scot-free. I am for striking out, but first we've got to think of food."

"Lije and Saul will go after deer. There are no better hunters in these parts. With what they can kill and what we have, we can get by for a few days. Then I will go after food myself."

"You?" O'Hara demanded. "Where will you get food?"

"Blazer. I'm not going to take all that time, either. I'm going across country, across the broken lands."

There was dead silence. Runyon leaned forward as if to speak, then sat back, shaking his head doubtfully. Smithers broke the silence. "I'll go with you," he said.

"Man," Hight protested, "even the Injuns shy away from that country. If there was any way across, I'd say take it, but men have tried, and died trying."

"There were Indians one time, old Indians, who knew a way across, and I think I know how it can be done. If I can do it, I need be gone only a few days at most."

Trent looked over at Jesse. "Do you want to watch Cedar? You and Quince, takin' turns? Don't take any chances, but when they start to move this way, bring us word. You can take that chestnut of mine. He's a racer, and loves rough going."

Jesse Hatfield got up and slipped from the room, taking up his rifle as he left.

"Jack"—Trent turned to Moffit—"you get up in the Eye and keep a good lookout on the Cedar trail. If you see anyone coming, give us a call."

He mounted the buckskin and took the trail for his own place. He knew what they were facing, but a plan of campaign was shaping itself in his thoughts. If they sat still, sooner or later they must be wiped out or starved out, and his own people would lose heart. They must learn to strike, and they must teach Hale that he was vulnerable.

All was still around his cabin when he rode in. There had been tracks on the trail, and he was not worried, as his was a most difficult place to reach.

Leaving the buckskin ground-hitched, he went inside and loaded two sacks with food of various kinds. A couple of slabs of bacon, some beans, rice, and dried apples.

When he had slung them on a packhorse, he crossed to the nail where he kept his guns. For a moment he hesitated. Then he took them down and buckled the gun belts about his hips. Matters had gone too far now, and the time for peace was gone. He stood for a moment looking around the quiet room.

Lonely it undoubtedly was, but there was a peace and a stillness here that meant much. How many times he had sat watching the fire on his hearth, or sitting in the door and watching the shadows grow long over the meadow.

There were a half-dozen head of good saddle stock in the

corral, and he drove them out and started them down the trail toward the Hatfields'.

Jackson Hight was the last one to reach the Hatfields'. He came up the trail on a lathered horse, his face white with anger. "Too late!" he said. "They burned me out!"

He looked at Trent. "I tried, Trent, I honestly did, but there were six of them. I winged one, though!"

Smithers pointed off over the trees. They could see a column of smoke there. "O'Hara's place."

Jesse Hatfield rode in. "Two bunches comin'. They figure to get here about sunup. I overheard their talk."

"All right, Jesse, you get some sleep. You too, Jack. Parson, you and Smithers stand watch, and Quince, I want you and Bartram to ride with me."

"W'ar you all headed for?" Saul asked.

"Why, I was just sort of thinking about going to market! We'll need some groceries, so I thought we kind of might circle around and pay Leathers a visit."

"Count me in on that," Saul suggested.

"You get some sleep. The three of us will do it, and if we can't, four would be too many. You get some rest."

"I ain't so wearied from chasin' antelope that I can't take the ride," Saul insisted. "It's a bad town, and I can surely make myself useful."

"All right, then," Trent yielded. "I'll not deny we can use you."

There was a burst of light off to the south, then smoke, scarcely visible against the darkening sky. "There goes my place," Smithers commented ruefully, "and I had a good crop of potatoes comin' up, too."

"Don't worry about them," Trent replied. "I'll help you dig them when this is over."

Smithers watched the four men ride away, and shook his head. "He surely makes you believe, doesn't he? Somehow his just saying that makes me feel better."

Parson Hatfield took his cold pipe from his teeth and commenced to tamp it. "He means what he says, Smithers, and when he gets around to telling you who he is, you'll have more cause for believing him. There rides one of the most dangerous men in the country, and from all I hear, he never looked to be, it just come up on him."

"Maybe we can win, after all," Smithers said. "Parson, let's go in and have a cup of coffee."

SEVEN

Trent led the way at a fast trot. The trail they took was a little-known game trail Lije Hatfield had located that led down off the mountain through aspen groves and into the pines. They rode cautiously, pulling up now and again to listen, and carrying their rifles in their hands for ready use.

They saw no one. It was a wild and broken country they came to finally, with great boulders everywhere and scattered cedar. The town lay not far away now but was still invisible.

Trent slowed the pace with more and more frequent stops. Their success depended on their getting into town unseen. Many of Hale's riders would be out looting and burning, and others would be sleeping. At this hour the town should be quiet. The Mecca and the Crystal Palace closed their doors at two in the morning, so all should be easy going if they took no chances.

Drawing up on a small knoll with the town below them, they could see only two or three lights. None of these were along the street except for one light in a room in the hotel where some drummer sat late over his accounts or perhaps over a dime novel.

Trent chose dusty lanes where a hoof would be unlikely to strike a stone, and he led the way past barns and corrals, weaving a careful way through outlying dwellings and garden plots toward the main street. Long since, knowing upon what a slender thread his existence hung, he had taken the time to notice these streets and lanes, mapping every exit in his mind.

He had also taken note where the barking dogs were apt to be, and his route avoided them. There was always the risk that some late rider might come upon them or some householder might step outside in time to see them.

King Bill, secure in his power, would never suspect the nesters of trying to enter his town or approach his ranch. He

42

would be expecting them along the overland route to Blazer, and without doubt that was observed. That they would ride right into the heart of his domain, he would never believe.

"Bartram," Trent whispered, "you and Saul take the packhorses behind the store. Keep them quiet, but don't try to get into the store or anything. If something goes wrong and there's shooting, get out of town, and get fast. Don't worry about us. It will be every man for himself."

He turned in his saddle. "Quince, we're going to get Leathers."

"Why not just bust in?" Saul asked. "We can find what we need."

"No," Trent said, "he's going to wait on us, and we are not only going to pay him but we are going to get a signed receipt. We are not thieves. There will be big trouble over all this, and when inquiries are made, I want us to have coppered every ace. Let him do the unlawful things, we'll stick to the safe side and be able to show we did.

"We will get him down here and we will pay cash on the barrel head for everything we get."

Leaving their horses with the others, they soft-footed it to the storekeeper's home, not over a hundred yards off. Quince, big as he was, moved like a ghost through the night, and several times Trent had to look around to make sure he was actually with him.

There was no moon. There were stars, and a few scattered clouds. The store buildings along the street were ominously dark against the sky.

Reaching the white picket fence around Leathers' home, he did not make the mistake of opening the gate, which would probably creak, but simply stepped over the fence.

There was a faint smell of lilac in the air, and the grass was damp. They paused when in the shadow of the porch and listened. A mockingbird sang interminably in a tree across the street, but there was no other sound.

Ever so gently he lifted one foot and put it down carefully on a step. Lifting himself with the muscles of the other leg, he took up the other foot and put it down cautiously. There was no sound. Inch by inch he worked his way across the porch and into the house.

Two people slept inside, Leathers and his wife. His wife was a fat, comfortable woman, and was one of those who idolized King Bill Hale. To her he was all a man should be, and she was much impressed by his swagger, his grandiose manner, and his style of living. He was, she was convinced, a great man.

Once, shortly after his arrival in Cedar, Trent had been in this house. He had come to get Leathers to return to the store, as he needed supplies after-hours. As his was a large order, Leathers was pleased to comply. Therefore Trent had some knowledge of the layout of the rooms.

The door he now opened gently was to the kitchen; from there a door led to a hallway, and from it a door to a living room, rarely used, and the bedroom. In that room Leathers would be sleeping with his wife.

Once inside the kitchen, he paused. Leathers kept a cat, but no dog, for which he was profoundly grateful. He moved quietly into the hall and paused to listen to the breathing in the next room. He could distinguish the slow, heavy breathing of Elsa Leathers and the jerky, somewhat erratic breathing of Leathers himself. The kitchen and the hallway smelled faintly of onions and homemade soap.

Drawing a large handkerchief from his pocket, he tied it across his face. Leathers would soon know who he was, but he hoped the immediate shock of a masked man would keep him silent. Then he slid his six-gun into his hand and stepped through the door into the bedroom. For an instant Elsa Leathers' breathing caught, hesitated, then continued. He heaved a sigh of relief. If she awakened, she would surely start screaming and all his carefully worked-out plans and his long ride would go for naught.

Alongside the bed he put the cold muzzle of the gun under the storekeeper's nose. Almost instantly his eyes opened. Trent saw the man's eyes turn toward him, then focus on what must be only a tall black figure in a flat-brimmed hat, masked and with gleaming eyes and a pistol.

Trent leaned down and whispered, "Get up quietly!"

Very carefully Leathers eased out of the bed. Trent gestured for him to pull on his pants and the slippers that lay alongside the bed. Then he indicated the door. Ever so softly, Leathers preceded him through the door.

Once outside, he turned on Trent. "What's the matter? What d' you want me for?"

"It's just a matter of groceries. You open your store and give us what we want, and you may live until morning. In fact, you step light and do what you're told, and you won't have any trouble at all. Make one squawk, and I'll bend this six-shooter over your head."

"Take it easy, now! I ain't going to say a word. Just you hold off, now." He buckled his belt and hurried toward the store, with Trent and Quince at his heels. Quince paused only long enough to pluck a blue cornflower from the garden and tuck it into an empty buttonhole of his shirt.

Leathers fumbled with the lock on the store door. "If my wife wakes up and finds me gone, I ain't responsible for what happens."

"Don't worry over it," Trent replied coolly. "You just fill this order as fast as you can, and no monkey business. And you'll lose nothing by it. I want an itemized list, and I'll pay you for every cent of it."

"You mean this isn't a robbery?"

"No." Trent pulled down the handkerchief. "I am simply buying supplies. It isn't a robbery, and it won't be a shooting if you hurry!"

He motioned to Saul, who came forward. "As soon as you an' Bart get four horses loaded, you let Bart take them to the trail. Then, even if somebody shows up, we'll have a part of what we need. You stay, and then leave with the next four."

"What about you and Quince?" He gestured toward his brother, who was standing just inside the door keeping an eye on the street.

"We'll follow and cover your retreat. We will be right behind you."

Leathers worked swiftly. There was a dim light from a lantern he lit in the back room, but not much was needed, as Leathers knew the location of everything. Nor was Trent worried about what he might do. The man was frightened, and they represented the immediate danger, Hale only a later danger but one that might be explained away.

As fast as Leathers put out the supplies, Saul and Bartram packed them on the horses. They worked swiftly and silently.

"You ain't goin' to get away with this!" Leathers protested. "When Hale finds out, he'll be right after you."

"Maybe he will," Trent said quietly, "but he'd better wait until he gets over one beating before he starts hunting another.

"As for that, you'd best start making plans."

"Plans for what?"

"When this fight is over and Hale loses, which he will do,

what about you then? What d' you suppose will happen to you?"

"What?" Leathers stopped, startled and suddenly frightened. "What do you mean?"

"I mean, my friend, that you've taken sides, which you need not have done, and if Hale loses, you leave. You leave with whatever you can carry in a buckboard, but you leave."

"He won't lose!" Leathers put a sack of beans on the counter, which Saul took from under his hand. "Hale is the boss here. He has the men and he has the money. Look at what happened today. Smithers' place gone, and O'Hara's, too. And look what happened to Dick—"

"Moffit?" Trent's tone was harsh. "What can you call that but murder?"

Leathers shook his head. "It wasn't—"

"What would you call it? An unarmed family man with two youngsters, a man on his own property. How can you be sure they won't someday decide to kill you? Moffit wasn't fighting. You knew him. He was a decent man, an honorable man."

Shaken, Leathers struggled for words. "I wasn't there," he protested. "I don't know what happened. You don't either."

"His children were there. They saw it all. We have two witnesses who can hang Cub Hale and those with him. And his father for ordering it, or at least conniving in it."

Quince stepped back inside. "Two men coming!" he whispered.

"Let 'em come in. No shooting unless they shoot first."

Trent stepped into the deeper shadows behind Leathers. He put a gun in the storekeeper's ribs. "If they come in, you just answer quietly. If there is any shooting, Elsa Leathers is going to be a widow!"

Two men came up to the door and turned the knob. As the door opened, one of the men asked, "Who's there?"

"It's me," Leathers said, and, prodded with the gun barrel, he added, "fixin' an order that has to get out early."

The two men came on in. "I never knew you to be up this early before. It must be four o'clock!"

"Right." Quince stepped into sight. "You invited yourselves to a party, so you can just start carrying those sacks outside."

"Huh?" The two men stared stupidly. "Why . . ."

Quince prodded the man with his rifle muzzle. "Move! Get those packs outside. Quick, now!"

It was growing gray in the east when all the horses were packed. Bartram had been gone for some time and should be well along the trail by now. Quickly they hog-tied the two men and then Leathers, gagging all three. From his pocket Trent took money to pay for what they had taken and tucked it into Leathers' pocket; then he released Leathers' right hand long enough to sign the receipt.

Saul started with the second batch of packhorses, and Quince mounted, rifle in hand. Trent picked up Leathers, and walking into the house, less quietly this time, placed him on the bed beside his wife. Elsa sighed heavily and turned in her sleep, but she did not awaken.

Trent waited an instant, then tiptoed outside and stepped into the saddle. They walked their horses down the lane, turned past the corral and the shadow of two barns, and disappeared into the trees.

"Leathers was scared," Quince said, "but by the time his wife wakes up and cuts him loose, he'll be sore as a boiled owl!"

"There will be a chase," Trent said, "so let's let them get up on the trail with the packhorses."

At an opening in the trees he glimpsed Bartram several miles ahead and higher up the mountain. Bartram was a tough, wiry young farmer and woodsman who had spent three years convoying wagon trains over the Overland Trail before he came north to settle on his own place. He knew how to handle a pack train and showed it now.

"You paid Leathers?"

"Yes, I did. And I have his receipt."

Using every device they knew to cover their trail, they moved steadily into the mountains.

Several times they paused to look back but saw no sign of pursuit. Trent got down from his horse and stretched. He doubted if anyone else knew this trail or would find it, and he hoped it would simply be assumed they had taken the regular road. Neither of the two tied-up men had seen the packhorses, and since the horses had been well to one side in the shadows, he doubted Leathers had. All there would be to see would be a confused pattern of hoof prints, and the immediate assumption might be that they had used a wagon. There were always plenty of wagon tracks on the road.

Trent walked back and dusted a few handfuls of dirt to blur their tracks and scattered some leaves. Then they rode on. They were still several miles from the Hatfield place when they heard distant shots.

Quince reined in. "They've attacked our place, Trent. Should we leave this to Saul and Bart and ride on in?"

Trent considered it, then shook his head. "We will trust to your pa and the others. We will just take our time with this grub. It's needed, and we daren't lose it."

They started on. The occasional shooting was a relief, for obviously the place had not been taken. Trent was only a little worried. Nobody was going to tree an old he-coon like the Parson that quick.

"Somebody comin' up the trail," Quince said. "Turned into it back yonder a ways."

"Trying to outflank the Parson," Trent said. "Saul? You keep going, but watch out for the attackers. They are trying to scout a way around your place. We'll handle this."

Saul wheeled his horse and started up the trail after the pack animals. Trent, taking a quick look around, led the way into a nest of boulders slightly above the trail. Riding up, they swung down and hid their mounts among the cedars. A good place for the horses and a good place to get away from if necessary.

The riders were coming fast now. Something must have alerted them, or they were sure they had found a back way into the Hatfields', which in fact they had.

Waiting, behind the boulders, Winchester in hand, Trent could hear them coming. A hundred yards away they suddenly broke into sight around a bend of the trail.

"Dust 'em!" Trent suggested, and fired.

The two rifles went off with the same sound, and dust leaped up in front of the nearest horse. Startled, the horse reared up and turned halfway around. Trent hesitated, to note the effect of their shots, then aimed high and saw the sombrero of one of the riders go sailing into the brush. The men whipped their horses around and disappeared down the trail.

Quince chuckled, then bit off a chew and tucked his plug of tobacco into his shirt pocket. "That will give them something to worry over!

"Say!" he exclaimed suddenly. "What'll you bet one o' them ain't shinnyin' up amongst those rocks yonder?"

There was a notch in the rocks, and they could see a boulder beyond, not four feet beyond, by the look of it. Quince lifted his Kentucky rifle and fired into the notch. There was a startled yell, then muttered curses. Quince chuckled.

"They won't try that again." Quince glanced over at Trent. "But we got to get out of here."

"I know. You keep them under cover and I'll ride around and get up yonder against the sky. Once I'm up there, I can drive them out and you come on up."

He was gone in an instant. Mounting, he rode down into an arroyo, working his way through the cedars until he could find a dim trail up into the tower of rocks overlooking the trail. It was a matter of minutes, and once in position, he left his mount and scrambled to a good position.

Now he could see the two men below, and he opened fire. He had no desire to kill either man, just to drive them from their position. His first bullet spattered them with flakes of granite, and they went scrambling from their now-exposed position.

Quince joined him a few minutes later. "They'll be slow showing theirselves again," Quince suggested. "We'll be nigh to home before they do."

They reached the trail again and rode on up the steep switchback trail, following the tracks of the pack animals. When they had ridden a good four miles, they came upon Bartram with the eight packhorses.

"Firing up ahead. Saul's gone on up to scout the situation. I'm holding fast."

Low-voiced, Trent and Quince explained what had happened, and they waited for Saul. Occasionally they heard a shot. In a few minutes Saul came down through the trees.

"Pa's got 'em stopped outside the Cup. I think only one man of theirs is down. I could see him lyin', all sprawled out. I reckon he's the only one who got into the Cup, an' you can be sure he ain't goin' out under his own power."

"Is there any way we can get these horses in?" Trent asked.

Saul nodded. "If'n you all can keep 'em worried over there for a bit, we can sure enough take 'em in."

"Consider it done." Trent fed shells into the magazine of his rifle. "When Quince and me open up on them, you boys hightail it in there. Then take shelter and cover us while we follow."

"Let's go," Saul said.

Quince opened fire, and with a whoop Saul and Bartram started the horses. Only one shot was fired from the other side, and it was high. Quince fired, and then Trent. After that the horses had disappeared and all was quiet.

The Hatfield place lay in a cuplike depression surrounded on three sides by high, rocky walls that leaned inward so there was no way to get atop them and fire down without risking a dangerous fall from the steep, smooth sloping rock atop the cliffs. On the other side there were scattered boulders.

There were two openings in the cliffs, one at the back of the house, the other at the side where they now were. Emerging from a split in the rock, they must race across open ground to the protection of the rock-walled barn and rock corrals. The house lay behind them.

Hale's men were scattered among the boulders, but they had been stopped there by Parson Hatfield and O'Hara.

From their present position they had two alternatives. They could make the break across the floor of the Cup, covered by fire from the house, or they could manage a flank attack on the men among the boulders.

Not more than five acres lay in the bottom of the Cup, a spot not unlike Trent's own, but farther down the mountain. There was here, as in his own place, a fine cold spring. However, if a rifleman could get up close to the front of those rocks, he could stop all movement in the bottom of the Cup. It was the weak spot of the stronghold.

Those men had to be dislodged, and it could only be done from where Trent and Quince now were. Leaving their horses in a sheltered position, they edged forward, Indian-style, until they could look down into the nest of boulders. There were a half-dozen men there, and they could see but one of them. Then another moved forward, and instantly Quince fired.

The man stumbled and fell. Got up, dragging a leg, and fell again, this time behind a boulder.

Trent saw a boot projecting from behind a rock and let it have one. There was a yell, and the boot disappeared. Trent could see what was probably the remains of a heel still lying on the rust-red rock.

Suddenly it dawned on the attackers that their position was no longer tenable, and as one man they fled. Quince put a shot among them to hurry them along, and Trent held his fire, watching.

A few minutes later they were mounted, riding away. At least one man was cursing at the pain of a wounded leg.

They waited, watching, but there was no further sound, no further movement.

"Drove 'em off, I reckon," Quince said, "but they'll be back."

"That they will," Trent agreed. "And we've got to get us a

man out in those boulders or up here where he can cover them."

Quince spat. "Trent, you're a good man, but you're showin' 'em mercy and they don't deserve it."

"You're right, and they don't. Trouble is, Quince, every man of them is alive. He's got his dreams, his hopes, his ambitions. Some of them have womenfolks who wait for them. A bullet is an end to all of it and I don't like to use that bullet unless I must."

"I reckon you're right, Trent, but they're comin' at us, we ain't a-comin' at them."

Trent got up and brushed off his pants. "When the time comes, I'll do what needs to be done, Quince, don't worry about that.

"Right now I think some of those boys are ready to draw their time and ride out of here. It's one thing to carry a gun and talk fight, it's another when the lead starts to fly and you know it can be you.

"Two of them are out of action, anyhow, and I think some of the others are having second thoughts. If it comes to that, I'll have to go get Dunn and Ravitz myself."

Quince glanced at him. "You reckon you could? The two of them?"

"I could, Quince. Indeed, I could."

"And Cub Hale?"

Trent hesitated. "He's another matter, another matter altogether."

EIGHT

When he thought about it, he realized he had never doubted his ability to beat another man. It was a part of his strength, he was sure. He was gifted with uncommon speed of hand, steadiness of nerve, and the ability to shoot instinctively. He sometimes aimed with a rifle, he never did with a six-gun. He just drew, pointed as he would with a finger, and fired.

Yet he was intelligent enough to know that no matter how good a man can become, there is always, somewhere, a better. And he had a weakness, a weakness that Quince had sensed at once. He had compassion.

It was a land and a time when gentlemen settled disputes with guns, just as they for centuries settled them with battleaxes, lances, or swords. It was a tradition, not peculiar to the West, but common the world over. Perhaps someday it would end, but it was here now.

In Italy in one decade no less than 2,759 duels had been fought, most of them with swords and rapiers. It was also interesting to recall that while at least thirty of the duelists had been military men, twenty-nine were journalists, and the others a mixture of all types, but at least four had been members of Parliament.

The Chevalier d'Andrieux had killed seventy-two men in duels, and it had been rumored that Alexander Keith McClung, a nephew of former Chief Justice Marshall, had killed over a hundred.

The settling of disputes with weapons certainly was not confined to the West. Although some men had sought a reputation of skill with weapons, most of them had not, but had acquired their reputations simply because their skill—if not their intent—had given them victory.

"Pa figures you for a man good with guns," Quince said, "an' Pa ain't often wrong."

Did it show, then, as clearly as that? But of course. He himself could almost invariably spot a man who was dangerous, some because of uncommon skill, some because of some innate quality within them.

Mounting, Trent and Quince rode side by side into the Cup and saw Parson and young Bartram come forth to meet them.

"You surely got supplies," Parson commented. "I don't know how you done it."

"Oh, Leathers didn't object too much. When I took him over to the store and showed him what we needed, why, he just laid it out, nice as you please. Most men can be right accommodating if they are instructed in the right way."

Quince grinned. "Trent taken that poor man right out of bed, never so much as woke his wife. I could almost have felt sorry for him."

"I'd like to be hiding somewhere to see what happens when he wakes up," Bartram said. "Or when she wakes up."

Parson Hatfield was pleased, smiling through his handlebar mustache. "Well, I reckon we won the first round. Sure was a sight to see them punchers dust out o' there when you boys opened up on 'em."

"Who was the man we saw on the ground?" Trent asked.

"No-good renegade they called Indian Joe. He was no more Indian than you." He chuckled. "I can't say 'no more than me,' because I've got Injun blood. They call him Indian Joe, but he surely ain't Injun, no matter what he is. He was a bad one, so when he wouldn't stop comin', O'Hara gave it to him, dead center.

"That grub you brought in will sure come in handy, Trent, but you an' me know it ain't goin' to last us long. We got a passel o' folks here, and they be good eaters."

Parson seated himself on the doorstep. "We surely can't go into Cedar and do that again. We've got to figure some other way."

"We need a few days," Trent agreed. "And we've got to get to Blazer, there's no two ways about it. I wish I knew what they were planning right now, because I—"

"You ain't been payin' much mind," Parson said. "You stay to yourself so much. If you was payin' attention, you'd know what he's about, and you'd know that we won't be havin' too much trouble these next two weeks."

"Why? What's going on?"

"King Bill has got him a big celebration planned. A carnival like. He's been in this here country ten years now, so he figures to pull off a big celebration.

"They're going to have horse races, footraces, horseshoe pitching for prizes, and there's to be a prizefight. Hale is bringin' in a bare-knuckle fighter called Tombull Turner. A big feller . . . good, they say."

"He is good. I've seen him fight. He's big and strong and mean." Trent thought about it. "Maybe that will give us the time we need."

He got up. "I'm going to get some sleep." He touched his face gingerly. "I'm still sore."

"Color on your eye is fadin'," Quince said.

Trent studied his hands, still puffed and swollen from the pounding he'd given Hale. "It's these that worry me, but they aren't as sore and stiff as they were."

He unrolled his blanket in a place where the afternoon sun would not disturb him. It was early, but he hoped to sleep right on through, and was tired enough. He lay down on his blanket and stared up through the leaves.

Tombull Turner! Hale certainly tried for the best. At least, the best in this part of the country, which meant anything west of the Mississippi and short of San Francisco.

Then his thoughts shifted to the problem of getting to Blazer. Several times, from vantage points in the mountains he had studied the country to the west and south, seeking a possible route. He had good field glasses, a relic of his Civil War service, swapped for from a German officer who was returning to his own country. They were excellent for the time, and far out in the rugged waste he had spotted what seemed to be a trail. Whether a game trail or Indian path, he knew not, but obviously a route used by someone, and long enough to have established a path. That meant the trail went somewhere, and he had learned the folly of leaving desert or mountain trails to begin his own, for often such routes were the only possible way through the mountains.

It was nearly dusk when he awakened. He lay still, hands clasped behind his head, trying to assemble his thoughts about the forthcoming trip. Blazer was only a crossroads, one of those places born to die and leave only a few splintered boards and broken glass to mark its passing. Yet for the moment its existence was crucial.

Walking to the spring, he drank long and deep, then bathed

his face; it was feeling less sore, and his jaw worked more easily, some of the stiffness having left it.

Sally brought him a rough towel with which he dried his face and hands; then, with the towel over his shoulder, he combed his hair, looking into a small piece of broken mirror nailed to a tree.

"Two more men came in," she said, "Tot Wilson, from down in the breaks near the Box Canyon, and Jody Miller, a neighbor of his'n.

"Jody's a Texas man. Used to ride the trail drives up to Kansas, and he's a good man."

Trent glanced at her, eyes twinkling. "How good a man? You interested in him?"

She blushed. "No, I am not! I . . ." Her voice trailed off.

"Yes?"

She blushed. "You'd better come and eat." She paused. "I hear you're sparkin' that woman who runs the Palace, down to Cedar."

He smiled at her as he finished combing his hair, watching her in the mirror. "We're old friends, Sally. I knew her long ago."

"Is she a good woman?"

He nodded. "Yes, she is. She inherited a saloon down in Texas and had to run it or starve to death. She had helped with the accounts a long time before and knew a good deal about it. So she has done well.

"Jaime Brigo owed her father a debt, so he appointed himself her bodyguard, and nobody wants any part of Jaime, so she gets along all right."

"She's beautiful. I saw her once on the street."

"Yes, she is, and she has an excellent mind. Very clear thinker." He picked up his hat. "Sally, you've a good mind, too. Don't let it go to seed. A brain is only as good as you give it a chance to be, and just as important to a woman as to a man."

Saul looked up as they entered the house. He indicated the two strangers. "Wilson an' Miller, both burned out. They killed Wilson's partner. Shot him down when he went to rope a horse."

Miller was a stocky, solid-looking man, unshaved for several days. His beard was black and his eyes also. "Hi," he said. "I've seen you before."

"I've been places before," Trent replied mildly. This was it. He could tell by the expression in Miller's eyes.

"I'd have known you even if it wasn't for that big fellow down in Cedar."

"What big fellow?" Trent asked.

"Bigger'n you. He rode in about sundown yesterday askin' about a man fittin' your description. Wants to find you pretty bad."

"Flat face? Deep scar over one eye?"

"That's him! Looks like he's been in a lot of fights, and bad ones."

"He was in one that I know of. That one was all he needed."

Cain Brockman!

Even before he heard from Lee Hall he had known this moment would come sooner or later. All that was almost two years ago now, but Cain wasn't a man who was apt to forget. He had been one of a hard-riding, fast-shooting pair, the Brockman twins, widely notorious on both sides of the border. In a fight down in the Live Oak country Trent had killed Abel Brockman, and later, in a hand-to-hand fight, had whipped Cain into a staggering, punch-drunk hulk. And now Cain was here, hunting him down. And Cain Brockman was a good man with a gun.

As if it were not enough to have King Bill Hale on his hands!

Parson Hatfield sat staring at Trent. "You say you know this man, Miller. I'd like to, my ownself!"

"The name," Trent said slowly, "is Lance Kilkenny."

"Kilkenny?" Bartram dropped his plate, startled. "You're *Kilkenny?*"

"I am," he replied, "although the reputation that goes with it is not one I've tried for."

Turning, he walked outside and across the clearing. He did not want to talk about being Kilkenny nor to answer the questions that might be asked. While he was gone, they could talk if they wished, and there were stories enough, most of them untrue.

Whenever the names of gunfighters were mentioned, his was sure to come up. John Wesley Hardin, Wild Bill Hickok, Billy Brooks, Cullen Baker, Bill Longley, Farmer Peel, John Bull, Bat Masterson, Luke Short, Long-Haired Jim Courtright . . . there was a legion of them, some alive and some dead.

Most of them followed the boom towns; some were gamblers and law officers combined, like the Earps; some had inflated reputations, like John Ringo, whose reputation was great when stories were told but hard to pin down when it came to names, dates, and places.

Ringo had been involved in the Mason County War in Texas and had served time in prison for it, had been involved in the killing of the Haslett brothers, storekeepers at Huachita, New Mexico, and in various robberies and ambushes, the killing of a man in a saloon who ordered beer when Ringo wanted him to drink whiskey (the man was unarmed), and other such incidents. It is very likely that had he stuck to his family name of Ringgold he might never have been heard of, but the name Ringo had a sound to it. And too bad, too, Kilkenny reflected, for he came of a good family.

Cain Brockman was here. The thought made him suddenly weary. It meant that sooner or later he must shoot it out with Cain. In his reluctance to face a shootout with Cain Brockman there was more than his dislike of killing. He had whipped Cain with his hands, and he had killed Abel when the latter was trying to kill him. It should be enough.

Morever, he had always felt that Cain Brockman, good as he was with a gun, might never have gotten into trouble had it not been for Abel. Left to himself, Cain was a hard-working man and a capable cowhand or trail driver. Without doubt he was hunting Kilkenny because he believed it his duty to avenge his brother.

If there was to be any killing here . . . His mind skipped past Dunn and Ravitz and centered on Cub Hale.

It was possible that Cub Hale was the evil genius behind all the trouble in this section of the country. Arrogant and self-loving as his father might be, Kilkenny doubted there was viciousness in the man. Except, he thought ruefully, when he was in a fight.

What would King Bill Hale do next? Without doubt the beating he had taken from Kilkenny had hurt his pride, and he might simply withdraw. This, Kilkenny did not believe. No, it was more likely that he would find some way of striking back.

It was not only the beating which would rankle, but the fact that the nesters he had sought to drive out had fought back and had driven off his men. Then the man called Trent or someone had come into Cedar and secured a large amount of supplies after he had ordered them refused.

The power of any man or any nation is founded largely on the belief of others in that power. To maintain leadership, Hale must win victories, and now on three occasions he had been defeated or set back. The answer seemed plain. Hale must do something to win back what prestige he might have lost. But what would he do?

Despite the successes of the nesters, Hale was still very much in the driver's seat. He was also in possession of all or most of the facts. He would know how many men they had, and he could make a fair estimate of the food required to supply them.

Hale could, if he were so minded, just withdraw his forces, put a strong guard across the trail to Blazer, and sit tight. Starvation would sooner or later put an end to resistance. Or he could attack again with greater force.

Kilkenny—and it seemed strange to be thinking of himself as Kilkenny again, he had used the name of Trent for so long— did not believe in the all-out strike. By now Hale understood that the Hatfields and those with them were strongly entrenched, and win or lose, he would lose more men than he could afford.

There was no good route from the Hatfields' to Blazer. There was a trail for riders, at best, and that one could be blocked off. Moreover, he had men of his own in Blazer and owned the livery stable there.

His thoughts turned to the Smoky Desert, which was a purely local name used only by the nesters themselves and picked up from an Indian who had called it that on one occasion. He refused to believe it could not be passed. In his time he had covered a lot of country, and there was always a way . . . or there always had been.

O'Hara walked out to where he stood. "Miller and Wilson want to try to get to Blazer. What d' you think of it?"

"Not much. I want to try, but I want to cross the rough country. I believe there's a trail out there that's been lost, but if we try the other route, Hale will be waiting for us, going and coming."

"Wilson said he tried the Smoky Desert route. Says it can't be done. There are deep canyons out there, and miles of bare rock."

Jackson Hight, Miller, and Wilson came over to him. "We've been talking it over, and we believe if we cut into the trail to Blazer this far up that it won't be watched. We think we can make it."

"It's up to you," he said finally. "I wouldn't send a man over that trail, but if you want to tackle it, you can."

He paused, looking down the slope through the trees. "The trouble is that Hale has many men and we have but few, and we can't afford to lose even one.

"I'd advise against it, and I think Hale will be waiting for you."

"This far from town?" Miller protested.

"One man can patrol a long stretch of that trail and just send a signal back. Hale is thorough, and you can bet he won't miss a trick."

He knew how they felt. None of them liked being cooped up here, waiting for Hale to make his move. Each had the desire to be doing, to be striking out.

"Go if you like," he said, "but go prepared to fight. They'll be waiting for you."

At midnight the wagon pulled out of the Cup. Miller was driving, with Wilson, Hight, and Lije Hatfield riding escort. Kilkenny was there to watch them go, and then he returned to his bed under the trees to sleep.

Twice during the night he awakened with a start, to lie listening for the distant sound of shots, but heard nothing.

At daybreak he was up. Sally and Ma Hatfield were making breakfast, and two of the younger girls were helping. Nobody talked; all listened from time to time at the door or near one of the open windows. They heard nothing.

"Maybe they got through," Sally suggested.

He shrugged. "Maybe."

When he had finished eating, he saddled up and rode out of the Cup. The Parson was at the entrance, and he looked up at him. "You be careful, Kilkenny."

"I will." He gestured down the trail. "I am not going far. I just want to read the sign."

He followed the dim trail of the wagon past the Moffit cabin to the Blazer trail. As he rode, he stopped frequently to listen. So far, the wagon was not followed, nor did he see any evidence that it had been seen.

Lije and Hight had been riding well ahead of the wagon, often as much as a half-mile ahead. Several times he saw where they had paused to wait for the wagon to come up to them, and once they had stood talking for some time before moving on.

Had they seen something? Heard something?

Suddenly the hills seemed to fall away before him, and he

sat his horse looking over a vast area of broken hills, canyons, folded rock, sheer rims, shattered along the top, its rock falling to long talus slopes below. The dim trail led down from where he waited, and disappeared into a fold of the hills.

There were no tracks, so that meant that somebody, probably Lije, had thought of leaving none. Blazer was not far, yet by the route they had taken it was doubtful that a wagon could make ten miles in a day, and every day on the trail increased the danger of attack.

There was nothing to be gained by following them. He turned his mount, a sturdy black, and started back to the Cup. On a sudden whim he turned off and rode through the trees by a devious route to the ledge from which he could look over what was called the Smoky Desert.

Actually, it was not a desert in the usual sense, and much of the time it was without the dust or haze by which it had won its name. Far below he could see the remains of a ruined wagon—a few boards and a wheel; there seemed to be another half-buried in the sand.

He rode slowly along the rim, looking for a way down. If some way could be found from where he now sat his horse, it would shorten the distance by half, for Blazer must be almost straight across the rough country. Most of the way the rim was a sheer drop for anywhere from sixty to a couple of hundred feet, and in every case that drop ended in a steep talus slope. These cliffs and canyons that lay farther out had caused the road to Blazer to swing in a wide semicircle, but the Indians said there had been a way, and he had learned to believe Indians when they said something like that. So he rode carefully, studying the lay of the land.

At places he got down from his horse and walked along, the horse following. Yet search as he might, it was almost noon before he found anything that resembled a way down.

It was scarcely three feet wide, so he found a place where the cedars cast some shade and tied his horse there. Taking his Winchester, he followed what seemed to be a path down through some great, tilted slabs of rock. The trail, if such it was, carried him out to the very edge, and when it seemed his next step must be into space, the trail turned sharply right along the very face of the cliff.

He hesitated, taking off his hat and mopping his brow. The path seemed to lead right along the face of the cliff, but was at times almost broken away where the edge had crumbled or been knocked off by a falling boulder. One thing was certain. This was no way to bring a wagon or even a horse. Yet he walked on, edging along the sheer face, working his way slowly down.

The end was abrupt. The trail simply stopped. An hour of walking had brought him to a dead end. If in some prehistoric time this had indeed been a trail, it had long since ceased to be one.

He had turned carefully to start back when his eyes caught something half-buried in the sand below. It was a wagon wheel, perhaps from the same wagon he had seen earlier.

There were vague indications of something that might at one time have been a road, yet he could see little of it, for it vanished under the bulge of the cliff. He drew back in a cold sweat.

It was a good three hundred feet to the bottom, and obviously someone at some time had had a wagon down there. But how had he gotten it there?

Had the shelf upon which the road had run broken off in a slide? Or an earthquake? Quakes were not infrequent, for he had experienced one minor shake since his arrival, and had heard of others from the old Indian who had told him of the way across toward Blazer.

Taking a point of black rock for a landmark, he retraced his steps. At once he realized that in his enthusiasm he had come farther than he expected, and also that the trail was much harder when one was climbing back up. By the time he reached his horse, he was tired, dead tired. He had walked about six miles, going and coming, and his boots were built for riding, not walking.

Yet there was a way down there, and there could be a way across the rough country between.

It was up to him to find it.

NINE

When Kilkenny rode into the Cup that night, Parson Hatfield looked up from the rifle he was cleaning. "Howdy, son! You look about done in!"

He swung down and stood for a moment beside his horse. He was dead tired, and his shirt, which had been soaked with sweat, now felt stiff and uncomfortable. For the first time he wondered if they really could win. Without food they were helpless, and he had no faith in the success of the few who had gone with the wagon. If they made it through without losing somebody, they would have to have more luck than a man is allowed.

King Bill Hale simply had too many guns, too much on his side. And without food and more ammunition, they could neither escape nor continue to resist. Including those who had gone with the wagon, there were fourteen men, six women, and nine children to feed here. It was too many.

That night they were on short rations. There was no complaint. Only on the faces of those women who had men gone with the wagon could he see any worry. And they had reason.

"Any sign from Hale?" he asked.

"He's got men out in the rocks," O'Hara said. "They aren't trying to shoot anybody. They're just a-watchin'. But they are there, all right."

"I doubt if he will try anything now until after the celebration," Bartram said. "He's planning on making a lot of friends with that affair, and he's invited some outsiders in. I think the last thing he would want right now is trouble."

Jesse Hatfield pushed back his torn felt hat. "I taken me a ride today. Done slipped out through the bresh and I got clean to Cedar 'thout bein' seen. I edged up close to town an' I could see a lot of work bein' carried on.

"They've built a reg'lar fightin' ring out in front of the livery stable near the hoss corral. Ropes an' everything. Lots of talk about Tombull Turner and whoever will fight him."

Kilkenny listened with only half his attention. He was remembering all he had seen that day; rested a little, with a few cold drinks of water and a good meal in him, he was having second thoughts. The problem nagged at him, and he had a distaste for leaving any task unfinished. He had set out to find a way to Blazer, and he did not wish to give up. After all, that wagon *was* down there, and it had no wings.

His thoughts were going along the rim, searching at every possible angle, trying for a way down. That old Indian, now— just what had he told him?

"This Dan Cooper was there," Jesse Hatfield was saying, "an' he was doin' a lot of talkin'. He said that Turner hadn't been brought here by accident, that he was here for just one reason. To whip Kilkenny!"

"Did he actually use that name?" Kilkenny's attention was arrested. "Do they know who I am?"

"He said Trent. I don't reckon they know."

Tombull Turner brought in to beat him? Kilkenny doubted it. In the first place, he was no prizefighter and had no intention of fighting anyone. He remembered the bullet head, the knotted cauliflower ears, the flat nose, and the hard, battered face of the man.

Tombull was a fighter, and what was more, he was a brute. He was an American who had fought much in the prize rings of England. He had met Joe Goss and Paddy Ryan, and he was good. Of course, he did swing too wide with his left.

Long ago, when Kilkenny had worked out with Jem Mace, one of the first men to bring science to the game, Jem had taught him to watch a man for faults. "We all have habits," he said, "me an' you as well as the others. Watch for the way a man moves, throws his punches, how he reacts when hit, how he advances, retreats, and sidesteps. Nobody does everything right."

Dan Cooper was indulging in idle speculation, no more. Trent was not in Cedar, and not likely to be, and with matters as they were, there was no communication between them.

Conversation died out, and the men sat still, smoking or simply daydreaming, or seeming to be. What they were all thinking of, Kilkenny knew, was that wagon on the road to Blazer.

They would have to rest soon. Rest the horses, no matter

how much they wished to go on. Hours out on the road with no
chance of support from anyone if trouble developed. They
were men alone, isolated, cut off.

The food and ammunition were necessary, but four men
were out there, four of their own, men who had shared their
work, their trials, and some of them had even come west with
them over the long trail from Kentucky or Missouri. Lije Hatfield was among them, and knowing the family, Kilkenny realized that if he were killed no Hatfield would rest until those
responsible had paid the price for his death.

Knowing the route, he could picture the wagon rolling along
over the rough, rocky way. Never a good trail, and used but
rarely, there was no chance to go quickly. And they must have
horsemen out to front and rear, watching, hoping, fearing.

If they were still alive and free, they were making a cold
camp now, for they would not dare to have a fire. They would
be resting, if lucky, and they would have their worries, for they
could not know that all was quiet with their families. What
they did know was that everybody here was depending on
them, needing their success. The little food brought back from
Cedar would last but a few days longer.

That night Kilkenny soaked his hands in brine. They were
better, but he wished to toughen them. His eye was open
again and the discoloration faded. In the high, cool weather
and fresh air, the cut had healed well, yet was still tender.

Sally came to him and watched him with his hands in the
brine. "What you doing that for?" she asked curiously.

"Bare-knuckle fighters do it to make their hands tough and
the skin firm. Some of them put it on their faces, too."

"Does it work?"

"I don't know. They all believe it does."

"Are you going to fight that man? Tombull Turner?"

"Of course not. Why would I? If I even went down there, I'd
be walking right into their hands. No, I just want my hands in
shape. A man never knows what will happen."

"Bart says Hale will never rest until he has you whipped.
Not only killed, but whipped."

"We don't know what he is thinking. Mostly, I think he just
wants us out of here."

"They say you've killed thirty men."

Irritated, he looked up. "I have never said that. I don't talk
about such things. Like some of the rest of them here, I was in
the army, and I did what I had to do. We were fighting to

preserve the Union. Since then there has been a little trouble here and there, but I never looked for it or wanted it, like here.

"Your pa—Dick Moffit—he didn't want it, but they brought it to him. A man must defend himself or die."

"Do they use guns so much back east?"

"Almost as much. Remember, it was only a few years back that Andrew Jackson killed a man in a duel. Then, there was the Hamilton-Burr affair. Alexander Pushkin—he was a Russian poet—was in a number of duels and finally killed in one. I don't like it, but that's the way it is."

On the morning of the third day after the wagon left, Kilkenny mounted and started for the rim. He caught Parson watching him, but the old man offered no comment.

This time Kilkenny had a plan. He was returning to the place he had been before, and by one means or another he was going down the face of the cliff to the ruins of the wagon; then he would try to discover how the wagon came to be there.

It lay much too far out to have ever fallen from the rim, so there had to be a trail. Once down there where it was, he could either find something of the trail down which it had come, or by backtracking and search from below, he could find the route it used.

If he could find no trail, he would have to get back up a cliff that was at least three hundred feet high, but that was a bridge he would have to cross when the time came. He was taking a long chance, but if ever there was a time for risk-taking, it was now.

Somewhere in that vast jumble of broken cliffs and canyons, fallen slabs, and shoulders of stone he would find a way down.

It was almost seven o'clock in the morning when he reached the point where he planned to descend. He had brought along several ropes, not enough to reach the bottom but enough to get him to the steep talus slope down which he could make his way.

Lying flat, he peered over the edge. At this point the cliff bulged out somewhat, and he could not see the bottom immediately below, but he hoped to swing back in against the cliff face, where he could use roots or projections of rock to help in his descent. He was no mountain climber, although he had once read something of their methods in an old magazine, *Atlantic* or *Century*, he believed. He wished he could review it now, for he would need all the help he could get.

Forcing himself to think of nothing but the task at hand, he lowered himself over the edge, and when he got the merest toehold, he felt below until he could grasp one of the roots, and slowly eased himself lower.

The depth below was sickening, and he had never cared much for high places. He had made fast his rope to an ancient gnarled and twisted cedar near the edge, and had run the rope between his legs, across his chest, and over the opposite shoulder, then across his back, gripping it in his right hand. In this way he could lower himself carefully, occasionally guiding himself with his left hand.

Resolutely he kept his thoughts away from the vast depth below, but in a matter of minutes he was wringing wet with perspiration. He lowered himself slowly, but the rope was burning his skin right through his clothes. He slid, held himself, and grabbed a projection of rock and felt for a toehold on the wall. For a moment he was still.

He dearly wanted to wipe the perspiration from his face. It trickled into his eyes, which smarted from the salt sweat. He glanced to the right along the face of the cliff, and far off in the blue he saw a buzzard swinging in lazy circles.

His fingers ached with gripping, and he released his hold on the rock and let himself slide down some more. If an enemy discovered him now, he would be cold turkey, no chance to even fight back. The slightest slackening of grip on his right hand and that rope would be gone and he would be falling.

He needed to ease the weight again. His toe found a rock, tested it. Solid. Slowly, carefully, he began to settle weight on the ball of his foot. Suddenly there was a sag in the rock beneath him, and it gave way and the rattle of falling stones told him he had lost that toehold.

Slowly he lowered himself again. What in God's world was he doing here, anyway? This was a damned fool thing . . .

The rope slipped and burned through his hand, across his back. He gripped it hard and regained control. If he just had nerve enough, he might lower himself all the way down without trusting to foothold on the cliff face, but he was wary of it, afraid of going too fast.

He glanced up. He had come down at least fifty feet, and perhaps farther. If he quit now, he could climb that distance hand over hand, but if he went farther, he doubted he would have the strength to climb back.

He lowered away, got his toe in a cleft of rock, looked to

right and left. Nothing. He lowered away again, and the rope grew hot. He waited, his left hand clinging to a root, and glanced to the right. A cedar grew there from a cleft in the rock, and beyond was a series of tracks. He glanced down. Fear tore at his guts. He clung for a moment, thinking desperately. He had underestimated the distance, for looking down from above, it was not easy to judge, and he was almost to the end of his rope, with a good forty feet to go, over jagged rocks, then the talus slope of smaller broken slabs.

If he could swing over to that cedar . . . It was a good, strong-looking tree, not more than four feet tall but almost twice that across, with thick, strong branches. Such a tree might be several hundred years old, for they had a fantastic ability to survive. Below it, there were several other trees, the nearest a good ten feet lower down.

Yet, if he could get over there, get his fingers in those cracks, he might make his way to the bottom. The distance to the head of the slope was about the height of a four-story building.

If he could start himself swinging, and at the farthest point of his swing cut the rope, he had a good chance of landing in that cedar.

And a better chance of missing and breaking his fool neck.

He pushed against the rock, tried to get himself swinging across the face of it. A push here, another there, and he was swinging like a pendulum. With his free hand he got out his knife. It was a good blade, and razor sharp.

Could he cut through in one slice? That knife would cut through anything, but . . .

He swung wider and wider, a great human pendulum against the face of the rock. The cedar was there; then he was away from it. It was a good rawhide riata, and he hated to sacrifice it. He let the swing reach its full distance, and when he neared a projecting rock, he shoved hard with his feet; the swing of the rope carried him farther over each time, yet scarcely far enough.

Could he cut through the rawhide with one slash? The answer was simple. He had to. Again he reached the far end of the swing. With feet and hands he shoved off hard from the rock; then his body swept out in a long swing over the breathtaking depth below. There was an instant of rushing air; then the cedar was there, just below him and ahead. Raising his left arm, he saw the cedar there and cut down and across with a sweeping slash.

He felt himself falling, and then he was thrown rather than fell into the cedar. He hit the tree all doubled up, and the short, stiff branches ripped at his clothes like stabbing knives. He fell through the outer branches and hit the second tree well below. For an instant the branches seemed to hold him, and then he slipped through and fell again. He hit a bunch of brush and was dropped off the edge of it to the slope. He hit the sand, rolled a few times, and lay still.

After a long, long minute he pulled himself together. He glanced up and could see his rope dangling there, so far above him that he could not believe it. Gingerly he felt of arms and legs to see if all was intact. Aside from a few minor bruises, contusions, and scrapes, he seemed all right.

Now he was down. How he was to get back to his horse and rifle was another thing.

He turned and began to walk.

TEN

Lance Kilkenny stood on a dusty desert floor littered with slabs of rock obviously fallen from the cliff above. He stood in a dry water course, or on the edge of it, along which water actually ran only during or after rains. Yet the first thing he saw other than that was immediately reassuring. It was an ancient Indian petroglyph.

It was on the face of the cliff thirty yards away, but clearly visible, although the colors had undoubtedly faded. It had been painstakingly pecked out of the rock, as he could see as he walked closer, and then tinted—or so it appeared.

Indians, at least, had been here.

To the west, vision was obscured by dust; it was a fine dust set swirling by the least wind. He knew nothing of what lay out there except that beyond a part of it lay Blazer. The first thing was to find that broken wagon.

His guns, which had their rawhide thongs over them, had stayed with him. His knife was lost. Or was it? Certainly it had fallen after he lost his grip on it when he cut through the rawhide.

He scrambled back up over the rocks and looked along the base of the cliff.

The knife was easy. The bright steel blade caught the sun and flashed brightly. He walked to it, picked it up, and then, when he turned to retrace his steps, he saw about twenty feet of his rawhide riata, the part that had been wrapped about him when he fell. He retrieved it with the awareness that a man never knew what would be necessary, but as he did so he suddenly realized he was without water.

On the mountain above, that had presented no problem, for there were frequent springs and small streams that ran from under the slide rock toward the crest of the ridges. Here there seemed to be no water.

69

The particles of dust in the air seemed largely to be silicate and finer than sand.

He slipped the thong from his right-hand gun.

He stepped over the bleached bones of an ancient cedar and walked on. From behind a dry desert bush he glimpsed the white rib cage of a horse, and he walked over to it. The dry, curled leather of a saddle lay near it, a very old saddle of a make he was not familiar with. Men had come down into this country from Canada long ago, as early as or earlier than Lewis and Clark.

Sweat rolled down his face, and the thick dust rose when he walked. It was hot, very hot. He looked about for shade, but there was none. The face of the cliff was like a great reflector sending the heat back into his face.

It was very dry. He paused; removing his hat, he mopped the hatband, then put it back on his head and slipped the thong under his chin. Dust arose in little puffs at every step.

Twice he glimpsed whitened bones, those of a bighorn sheep, and again of a deer. He saw no tracks, nor did he see anything alive. He looked up at the sky, partially obscured because of dust, and he could not see the buzzard.

Nothing that lived . . . not even a lizard.

Suddenly he saw the wagon wheel. Weathered by sun, wind, and rain, it was great and splintery, the iron rim rusted almost away.

A little farther along, the wagon lay, and another wheel half-buried in dust. He walked on. An old wagon. A cart, rather.

Yet somebody had been here, somebody who had found a way to get down the cliff with a wagon. Unless—the thought turned him sick when he thought of it—unless that wagon had come across the desert and had been abandoned here when no way could be found to scale the cliff.

That was a probability he had not considered. He stood there for several minutes studying the cliff itself. Higher in some places than others, in no place was it less than two hundred feet from the rim to the foot of the talus.

He walked on. It was hot. Dust and sweat made his skin itch. Several times he turned and looked back. Only pits in the sand remained of his footprints.

Ahead of him there was a jutting promontory of rock where the cliff thrust out into the desert.

How far had he come? At least a mile, perhaps a half-mile

more. The promontory was at least a mile ahead of him. He walked on, wishing he had a drink, and alert for any sign of water.

One thing he realized at once. Crossing this country looked to be a frightful job. Where the sand was not heaped in drifts there were areas of bare, wind-worn rock, often tilted so badly that men might have to resort to what the Mormons had called "dugways," cutting a rut for the upper wheel so a wagon would not tip over when crossing a steep side hill. That meant slow, painstaking work.

He came upon the track suddenly. He had reached the promontory and rounded it, and there it was before him. Not a road, certainly, but at least a place where wagons had gone. The edges of ruts cut into the surface were visible, although most of the way they were filled with dust.

The wagon track came down off the cliff in a steep, winding trail down which no wagon could have come without some kind of a brake, a line perhaps that was fastened to the rear axle and then paid out gradually to keep the wagon from overrunning its team. Although the team might have been taken down separately.

He turned at once and began to climb. His mouth was dry, and he wanted a drink, and while there might be water down here, he knew there was water up there in the forest. Several times he stopped to roll boulders from the trail, and once he worked for half an hour with main strength, as well as crude levers made from broken limbs, in an endeavor to roll a big log out of the way. He succeeded at last, and had the satisfaction of seeing it fall, bounding from rock to rock until it splintered in several pieces.

Sweat ran down his face in rivulets, and his face and the backs of his hands were covered with a fine gray alkali dust. He walked on, leaning into the climb, for the trail was steep. Twice he paused to catch his breath and to look back.

He could see a dim streak heading generally westward, which was the trail, or what he called such. Yet, they could get a team down here, and with luck they could cross. They would have to carry water for themselves and the stock, at least on the first trip. There might be water out there; yet, if there was water, it would probably be alkali.

He went through a deep, shadowy cleft for perhaps a hundred yards, then started to climb again. Suddenly he came out into the sunlight and stopped abruptly.

At once he saw why he could not find the trail from above.

Across it, directly before him, and almost on the place where the trail turned off the cliff's top, lay a huge pine. Perched on the edge of the cliff, its roots weakened no doubt by rock falling away from them, the gigantic tree had blown down and fallen right across the trail. Around it, other pines had sprung up, until it was surrounded by a thick stand of trees that gave no hint of the road that lay beneath them.

The younger trees were none of them older than ten to twelve years, so the road could not have been used in that time. No doubt it was some early effort by pioneers or by gold seekers, long abandoned.

He crawled over the fallen giant and went through the grove around it. Then he started the trek back to where he had left his horse.

It was dusk by the time he reached it, and the horse seemed as pleased to see him as he was to see it. He pulled the picket pin and led the horse to the tree where he had cached his saddle. When he was saddled up he checked his Winchester, then wiped his guns free of dust and tested the action.

He walked the horse to a tiny rivulet that ran down from the mountain ridge and let him drink. Upstream, he lay down and drank deep of the clear, cold water. He had tasted nothing better.

While the horse drank, he picked a few wild raspberries and thought about what he had seen. If the trail was practical, they could cross to Blazer in one-third the time needed to take the roundabout route. And they would find no Hale guards watching this route.

He stepped into the saddle and turned toward the Cup. Two or three good men with axes could open a way through that grove and the tree that lay across the way.

Someday he would have to find out where that road came from. For the moment he cared only where it went.

He shucked his Winchester and held it in his hand. This was good country, great country, and it was a place for men to live. It was worth fighting for.

He must bring Nita to this place. She must see for herself what was here. Yet the thought left him uneasy. To bring Nita here was to share with her something he loved. Before he could do that, he must decide what he wished to do.

Wished? He knew what he wished. He wanted Nita. He wanted a home, and he wanted it here. Yet the same old problem remained. He was a gunfighter, a man with a reputation, and sooner or later it would always catch up to him. Even now they knew who he was, and when this was over, if he conformed to the pattern he had established, he would ride on.

Yet, must he do that? Why not stay? The Hatfields were good people, and they accepted him. They had had their own gun troubles, back down the line as well as here, and they knew a man did not have to go seeking such things. This was a wild, new land and a place where a strong man had to stand for what he believed.

One could not yield to the lawless and the ruthless, or soon there would be no freedom. It was among men as it was among nations.

So . . . perhaps he could stay. Possibly there was a way to happiness for him as well as for others. Certainly, since he had first met Nita Riordan he had thought of no other woman, wanted no other.

He had a rival. King Bill Hale wanted her, and King Bill was a strong, handsome man. He was a man with a place in the community, a man with powerful friends in business and politics. She could reign like a queen in King Bill's Castle.

She seemed to be in love with him, Kilkenny. But was she? Or might she change?

Hale seemed a cold, hard man, yet what man sees another as a woman sees him?

The side of a man that he shows to a woman is often very different from that seen by other men.

Worry began to move through him like a drug. Nita nearby was one thing, but Nita belonging to somebody else was unthinkable. Especially he did not want her to belong to King Bill.

Hale wanted her, and regardless of what she might believe, he could bring pressures to bear if his own eloquence failed him. He was king in Cedar Valley and he had already shown his willingness to ride roughshod over others. Her supplies came in over a road he controlled. He could not only control her business, he could prevent her from leaving if he wished. Jaime Brigo was the one reason he might not succeed, but Jaime was but one man, no matter how cunning in battle.

This was a corner of the West off the beaten track. King Bill had made it a point to be both hospitable and friendly to all visitors and travelers passing through, although few of the latter came this way because it was a dead end. There was literally no place to go from Cedar unless to prospect the surrounding hills.

Farther north there was a scattering of cow or mining towns, each one more or less isolated and concerned solely with its own affairs.

In conversation with outsiders, King Bill would paint the nesters as rustlers, thieves, and white trash. Nobody could know more than what he said, and many of the people of Cedar felt about Hale as did Leathers' wife.

At the moment it was King Bill's lack of action that disturbed Kilkenny. Hale had been badly beaten in that fistfight, and knowing the arrogance of the man, Kilkenny knew he would never allow that to pass. Moreover, when he refused them supplies, they had come and taken them from under his nose.

All this would be discussed in private around Cedar. There would always be some who would suggest that Hale's power was slipping, that he was on shaky ground. Hale was shrewd enough to know this, and of course Cub Hale would be wanting action. Again Kilkenny found himself wondering how much of the violence came from King Bill and how much only from Cub.

There are those who use a cause to cover their own lust for destruction and cruelty. He who uses terror as a weapon does it from his own demands for cruelty and not because it succeeds, because it never has.

The killing of a strong man only leaves a place for another strong man, so is an exercise in futility. There is no man so great but that another waits in the wings to fill his shoes, and the attention caused by such acts is never favorable. Yet, such men as Cub Hale did not care. They wished to kill and destroy because it enhanced their own image in their own mind. Cub had grown up in his father's image, but with additional touches. He did not consider the law as applying to him, but only to those vague "others."

Was Hale planning to starve them out? He knew how many they were, how limited were their provisions, and he had fed enough cowhands to know what they would require and how much. He also knew that a strong man may endure much in the face of adversity, but few strong men could stand to see their women and children endure the same troubles. It was man's natural instinct, bred from the ages before men were even men, to protect the family.

Hale could control the trail to Blazer, but did he know of

the way across the wilderness country? Kilkenny doubted if anyone knew. Hale had been in the country but a few years, and Kilkenny doubted if any of the townspeople in Cedar had been around the country much longer. Hale had brought many of his hands with him, recruited the rest from drifters through the country.

Even Kilkenny himself did not know if the trail was passable. It was doubtful if Hale had even considered the possibility of such a thing, and Kilkenny had heard of it himself only through the casual talk of an old, old Indian who spoke no English.

Saul Hatfield walked down from among the trees as Kilkenny neared the Cup. "Everything quiet?" Kilkenny asked him.

"Surely is." Saul was frankly curious about the dust-covered Kilkenny. "Jesse took him a ride down toward Cedar. Says they sure are gettin' set for that celebration. Expectin' a big crowd. They say Hale's invited some bigwigs from over to the capital to come an' set by to watch."

From the capital? That was good thinking on Hale's part. It was good politics. Hale would entertain them royally, would show them how his ten years in the area had benefited the country, and perhaps casually mention the trouble he was having with rustlers who called themselves nesters. Men who were trying to take from Hale valuable land he needed for expansion.

Kilkenny knew how persuasive such a man could be, and he would entertain them like royalty, and the bigwigs would go away much impressed. King Bill knew how to impress such men with his power, his wealth, his influence. Hale undoubtedly had friends in the nation's capital, too, and he would not hesitate to use their names.

His audience would be friendly, well filled with food and wine, and he would give the officials the idea that all was well in Cedar Valley. When it eventually became known that he had eliminated those troublesome outlaws in the mountains, it would be accepted as a public service. What most officials wanted was not to be troubled. They preferred to hear that all was well among the citizens, and Hale would know this.

In that moment Kilkenny decided he must go to Cedar for the celebration.

But how? And if he did go, by what means could he secure the ear of the visiting officials? And would they listen to him if he talked?

As he rode on into the Cup, he went over in his mind every

possible way in which he might get into Cedar. His very appearance would invite trouble, and he would have to kill or be killed, which would defeat his purpose at the outset.

If he killed one of Hale's men, Hale would paint him as one of the problems he must cope with, but if he himself was killed, he would just be an outlaw eliminated, a troublemaker who had come to disrupt the celebration.

Somehow he had to get into town and get to those officials to at least present his side of the picture. Or rather, the side of the nesters in the mountains.

A carnival atmosphere would prevail. The officials might be anywhere, and even to find them would be difficult, guided as they would be by Hale or Hale's men. Yet there was, he realized, one place where they would be sure to be. They would be present, and in favored seats, for the Tombull Turner fight.

For the first time he began to think of Turner. He had seen the man fight. He was a mountain of muscle with a jaw like a chunk of granite, deeply set small eyes, his nose flattened by punches, his lips rather thick. He was a good fighter. You did not even get into a ring with the likes of Joe Goss or Paddy Ryan unless you were. The two times Kilkenny had seen Tombull Turner fight, the man had won, and easily. He could hit with terrific force and could take a punch and keep coming. He had faults, but what fighter doesn't?

Kilkenny rode down into the Cup and dismounted. Parson Hatfield walked over to him with O'Hara and Jesse.

"Looks like you've been places, son," Parson said, indicating the dust. "You surely didn't pick that up yonder in the forest."

"I've been down in the desert," Kilkenny said.

"The Smoky Desert?" O'Hara asked. "You mean you found a way?"

"I did."

"Could you get a wagon down there?" Jesse inquired.

"With a little ax work. We'd need about four good men with axes to work awhile before we tried a wagon. But whether a wagon could make it across is more than I could say. I found the remnants of a very old trail . . . hasn't been used for ten to fifteen years, and maybe much earlier. How much it was used, I don't know, but I'd say it had seen some use at one time."

"Where somebody else went," Jesse said, "we can go."

"How about gittin' across an' gittin' out?" Parson asked skeptically. "Many a trail starts out mighty good an' takes a body nowheres."

"You're right," Kilkenny agreed. He stripped the saddle from the horse, and then the bridle, turning the animal into the corral. He carried the gear into the stable and put it on the rack. "I'm going to try it. We will have to carry water with us, and we will have to tie cloths over our faces and the nostrils of the horses. There's a lot of alkali dust down there, and from where I looked, it was mighty rough country. We'd have to take a couple of shovels and at least one good pole we could use for a lever in case we get stuck. There's no way it is going to be easy."

"Leave us shorthanded."

"That it will. Hale has been leaving us alone, and I think he will until his celebration is over, but we can't count on that. We've got to be ready—really ready—all the time."

He paused. "If I can start soon, we might even bring the other wagon back that way. Sure as they get through to Blazer, Hale will have men waiting for them when they start back."

He walked back toward the house, suddenly realizing how hungry he was. He had eaten nothing since early that morning, and he had used up a lot of energy.

"Hale has all the time he needs. We do not. He can afford to sit back and let us eat up our supplies, and in the meantime he is playing politics with those men from the territorial capital and laying the groundwork to have no questions asked when he wipes us out."

Jesse sat down on the step. "Ain't nobody about to tell our side of it."

Kilkenny took off his hat and stripped off his shirt. He drew a bucket of water from the well and began to bathe the dust from his head and shoulders. The muscles ran like snakes under the tawny skin. "I may go down there and try to talk to them."

"You'd never have a chance," O'Hara replied.

"They'd kill you," Parson said.

"Not while those officials are there. Not if they can help it. And the last thing I want is a gun battle. We've got to convince them we are what we are, just good citizens trying to build homes in the wilderness, and that we have filed on our claims . . . as they can find out by checking."

"How are you going to get to them?" O'Hara asked.

"I don't know. I've got to think about that. He will have

them as houseguests at the Castle, and they'd never let me get within a mile of that place.

"If I stood around on the street or mingled with the carnival crowd, somebody would recognize me and they'd just block me off or take me out of there. They'd just watch their chance, slug me, pour whiskey on my shirt, and if any questions were asked, I would be just a drunk they'd put in jail to keep out of trouble."

"Then how will you do it?"

"I'll think of a way." He paused. "I'm going to the bunkhouse for a clean shirt, but I'll find a way, somehow, even if I have to fight Tombull Turner."

He walked away from them, and they stood looking after him. "Fight Turner?" Jesse said. "He's crazy. Turner's a prizefighter. He's not another Hale."

"Maybe," O'Hara said, "but did you watch Kilkenny move? He's like a big cat."

"He can fight some," Jesse agreed. "He surely whopped King Bill, an' he was supposed to be something."

"But Turner's a prizefighter! A man who makes his living that way!" Runyon had walked up. "I don't think there's anybody west of the Mississippi who'd have a chance with him. Anyway, they'd have somebody picked to fight him who could give him a fight."

"He wasn't serious," Bartram commented. "He was just talking."

"Maybe," Parson said, "but it would be one way of gettin' close to those folks from the capital. Anyway, that can wait. What we've got to think about now is gettin' to Blazer with a wagon."

Nobody offered a word on the fact that one wagon had already started. They all knew what a slim chance it was that their wagon would get through, let alone get back with their men alive.

"That desert country is right spooky," Jesse said. "I done looked over it from the rim a time or two. I never lost nothing down there."

"If there was a way across," Runyon said, "we'd never have to worry about starving out. King Bill couldn't stop us from getting across."

"He owns property in Blazer," O'Hara said. "He ain't a man to leave much to chance. He's coppered every bet."

"Nevertheless, if we could make it . . ."

"If anybody can, Kilkenny can," Parson said. "He sets out to do something, he does it. He never said a word about what happened today, but if you noticed, he come back with a length cut off his rope, and he taken three of them with him. I wonder how he ever made it down that cliff."

There was no table long enough to seat them all, and nobody wanted to wait, so when the food was dished up they took their plates and sat down wherever they could, leaving the table for the family.

They were eating when Kilkenny came in. He got his plate and went to the step outside the open door. Shadows were gathering under the trees, and he felt fresher since his quick and partial bath.

Bartram came out and sat beside him. "Look," he said, "I think that's a bad notion, you fighting Turner. The chances are they have somebody picked anyway. And how would you get a challenge to them? They'd shoot whoever you sent down."

Ma Hatfield, a tall, rawboned woman in a gray cotton dress, came to the door. "They wouldn't shoot me," she said, "and if need be, I'll go."

"It was a notion," Kilkenny said, "just a notion. But I'd surely like to know who they've picked to fight him."

Ma Hatfield refilled their cups and stood by with the coffeepot in hand. "I hain't been to town in some time," she said, "an' I'm a-frettin' to go."

She looked at Kilkenny. "They say you know that Riordan woman. Wouldn't she be likely to know who's to fight?"

"She would know. She seems to know everything. She probably knows who is to come here from the capital, too."

He looked up at her. "Ma, if you're serious, I'd really like to know two things. I'd like to know who is to fight Turner, and I'd like to know who it is that is coming down from the capital."

"Why?" Bartram asked. "Do you know somebody there?"

"Wish I did. No, I don't know anybody there, but there's a man named Halloran . . . he's a man who would go a long way to see a good fight. He's at the capital, or so I heard."

"Come daybreak," Ma said quietly, "I'll ride into town. I'll see that Riordan woman—"

"Nita Riordan," Kilkenny suggested. "She's a fine person, Ma. You'll like her."

"Hain't no matter, one way or t'other, but I'll see her an' find out what I can."

Runyon studied him. "You've got more on your mind than a fight, but d' you think you can whup him?"

"Tombull Turner? No. I don't think I can. Maybe. No, I certainly wouldn't bet any money on my chances, but if I could get in there with him, I'd get a chance to talk to those men from the capital.

"Look . . . I'd be in the ring. They would certainly be at ringside. I'd take a beating just to get to them."

"You take it," Runyon said, "not me."

ELEVEN

At daybreak Ma Hatfield was off to Cedar riding a sorrel mare, and Kilkenny and several of the others had ridden to the great tree that blocked access to the old road.

Kilkenny and Quince went to work on the big tree with a crosscut saw, while the others started on the small grove that had grown up around the fallen giant, clearing away the younger trees as well as the broken limbs of the big tree.

During a pause, Quince straightened and rubbed his back. "They should be there today. I hope they made it."

"They should . . . if all went well." He rested his own back, unaccustomed to the saw. "Do you know Blazer?"

"Been there a time or two. Man there named Soderman. Big, fat, an' mean . . . mean as all get-out. He's Hale's man. Got him a gunman around named Rye Pitkin."

"I know him. He's a two-bit rustler from the Pecos country. He's a fair hand with a gun—that's all, just a fair hand."

"There's another pair. Gaddis, and a sidekick of his called Ratcliff. If we get there, we can expect trouble."

" 'We'?" Kilkenny smiled at him. "You figuring on the trip?"

"Now, you don't think I'd let a youngster like you go t' town alone, do you? There's gamblin' an' women an' liquor of all kinds, an' such sinnin' you never heard of. No, sirree! I think I best go alongside of you to sort of guide you through the evils."

They worked hard for several minutes, and the Quince said, "The bore o' that ol' rifle o' mine surely needs cleanin', an' I figure there's no need to really clean it until I've done shot somethin' with it, so I'll just ride along an' fetch that rifle with me . . . just in case."

They worked steadily until too dark to see, and when they stopped work, the road was open wide enough for a wagon to pass through.

O'Hara, who had done the work of two men with his ax,

81

stood looking out over the wasteland. "You can have it," he remarked grimly. "She don't look good to me."

Returning to their horses, they rode wearily homeward, and nobody had much to say. Tomorrow they would make the effort, and with luck they would go through, but what of the first wagon? What of Lije and the others?

Ma Hatfield reached Cedar before noon. She had taken her time and a roundabout way, and when she rode into town nobody seemed to notice. She came up the back streets and rode at once to the back door of the Crystal Palace.

Tying her mule, she tapped gently. For several minutes there was no response, but there was a small rear window, and she was quite sure she was being observed.

She did not object. After all, she was a stranger and they had a right. After a minute the door opened, and a big man was standing there, a big man in black pants tucked into black boots, two heavy belts of black and two guns. He wore a pure white shirt and a black vest studded with gleaming bits that looked like diamonds.

"Come in, Señora Hatfield! You are most welcome."

"You know me, then?"

He bowed gracefully. "I am Jaime Brigo. I have seen you."

He did not say where or how, but he turned away from her and led the way down the hall to a door that was, she noted, set solidly in timbers that formed the frame. This was no ordinary door, and it would take a battering ram or an ax to break through, and then it would not yield easily.

He tapped on the door and it opened. Nita Riordan got to her feet. "Señora? I am pleased. Would you sit? Do you prefer tea or coffee?"

Ma started to say "Coffee" and then reflected that it had been ten years since she'd had a cup of tea. "Tea," she said, "and a mite of sugar, please."

"Would honey do? I prefer it and rarely have sugar around. Although," she added, "I believe they do have a little at the bar."

"Honey will do just fine."

Ma Hatfield had been looking at Nita Riordan suspiciously. She was, Ma admitted to herself, a handsome woman. Not more than twenty, she guessed, but mighty sure of herself. Moved graceful-like, too. Beautiful, too, no doubt about it.

Ma decided she liked the chair she sat in, and liked the room. It was, she guessed, what they called a sitting room, and through a door on the other side she could see a rolltop desk and a chair, like in an office.

"You run this here place your ownself?"

"I do, señora. When my father died he left me such a place, and it was all I had. It was run it myself or starve. I learned very quickly."

The tea arrived, carried by an old Chinese. He placed it on the table between them, and some small wafers. Ma looked at them warily. She had heard all sorts of things about such places as this, and that furriner, too. That yellow one. She'd heard about them.

Nita poured two cups, then handed one to Ma with a couple of the wafers on it.

"You are Señora Hatfield? You have some handsome sons, señora."

Well, now! Maybe they was and maybe they wasn't, but it was nice of her to say so. "They're good boys," she agreed. "A mite inclined to shoot too quick, but even so, they don't miss often, although that Saul"—she shook her head—"he had a dead bead on a big buck night afore last, and him not three hundred yards off. Missed him. Missed him complete! I d'clare, I was glad his ol' pappy didn't see it. It would have shamed him."

"What is it you wish of me?"

"Miss, Mr. Kilkenny, he asked me to find out two things. He's wishful to know who is to fight this here Tombull Turner, and he also wishes to know who is coming to Cedar from the capital."

"We uns heard tell that Mr. Hale, him they call King Bill, had invited some folks down from the capital. I think," she added, "the one he's most thoughtful of is him they call Halloran."

"Halloran? Yes, he is coming. I am not sure about the others. He invited several, and three accepted, and I know that Halloran is one of them."

"Good! Now, who is to fight this here Tombull?"

"It is a man named Sandoval. He is a Basque from over near Virginia City in Nevada. I know nothing else about him."

"Just as well. Kilkenny was thinkin' o' fightin' Tombull hisself."

"Señora, he must not even think of it! This man is strong.

Oh, so very strong! And he has had many fights. Please, you must not let him think of it!"

Mrs. Hatfield chuckled. "Ma'am, you surely don't know much about menfolks! Not, at least, the kind we got yonder in the hills. Why, I couldn't talk my old man or ary one of the boys out'n a fight, let alone that Kilkenny! He does what he pleases, and when he pleases, although I do say I never knew a nicer, kinder, or more thoughtful man in all my born days."

"Señora, you must not tell him, but they have talked of it. Cub—he is Bill Hale's son—he suggested it. He said they should rope and hog-tie him and bring him down here and throw him in there with Turner. I heard them talking, but King Bill stopped that talk very quickly."

"Kilkenny aint afeerd, ma'am. He'd fight him in a minute. Fact is, he's talked of it. He says he doesn't think he could beat Turner, but it would give him a chance to talk to Halloran."

Nita Riordan put down her cup. She looked at the work-hardened hands of the older woman and felt ashamed of her own. The lean brown figure in the faded gray dress and sun-bonnet. There was little that was feminine about her except for the way her fingers touched the fabric of the chair, the way her eyes yearned toward the pretty things. Yet Nita was wise enough to sense the deep pride in the woman and knew she dared offer her nothing.

"Señora, you must not be seen here. I think some of the men know you, and . . . well, there are some evil men here. Mr. Hale would not want a woman injured, but I cannot say so much for some of the others. You must go."

Ma finished her tea. "I'm obliged, ma'am. The tea was pleasant to the taste. Been a long time since I had any tea."

"Did you know that Lance likes it? I mean, Mr. Kilkenny. I wonder if you would take a couple of pounds to him?" The thought had come to her suddenly that this was something she could give, if she was wise in the way she did it. Lance would know at once what she intended. "I know he doesn't get tea very often, and he does like it for a change. Would you be so kind?"

"I would. If'n you're up to sendin' it, I'll surely carry it along."

Nita left the room, and Ma Hatfield relaxed slowly. It was a lovely room, such a place as she had dreamed of but never experienced, for in her nearly sixty years of life she had lived only in log cabins or sod houses, often with dirt floors. It was, she thought, downright elegant.

After a bit Nita returned. "Can you ride the trails after dark?" she asked.

Ma smiled. "I should reckon. I been ridin' mountain trails since I was knee-high. What's troublin' you?"

"There are some of Hale's men around, and they are drinking. When dark comes, I will have Jaime take you out the way you came. Besides," she added, "I haven't talked to another woman in a long time.

"You see, the women here think because I operate a saloon and gambling hall that I am not a nice woman. I think I am."

"I think you are, too." Ma was immediately defensive. "My boy Quince, he says you're a lady, and I reckon Quince is a judge."

For two hours they talked quietly. Ma told Nita of the troubles of raising sons in the wilderness and in the wild western lands. "This here," she said finally, "is the first time we've had us a chance to make it. We got us some good land up yonder, and some prime bottomland along some of the creeks, and the boys have worked almighty hard clearin' more land, fencin' with cut poles and the like.

"We done planted some fruit trees, and we got a good corn crop in. This year we put a floor in the house, and Pa's goin' to take time to make a new bedstead. He's a hand, Pa is, does most anything with tools. Quince takes after him. Lije, he cares mostly for huntin', trappin', and the like.

"We had too many boys for the small land we had back in Kaintuck, so Pa ups and comes west to Missouri. We had us a chance there, good rich land and hard work, and then the grasshoppers come and eat all our corn and we was left owin' for the seed.

"Next year we had floods and hail, and we didn't make a crop that year, either. We lost our land because we couldn't pay our bills, an' Pa moved to Kansas. There the Jayhawkers, Quantrill and them, they burned us out twice. The boys was all away at war but Saul, and Pa and him, they made a fight of it, me helpin'.

"We just lost everythin'. Pa, he's worked hard all his life, but we never seem to more than make ends meet. Pa had him some fine horses there in Kansas, but the Injuns run them off an' that was the time they kilt Grandpa.

"Then we come here and settled up yonder where we didn't

think we'd be bothered. We've done a sight of work gettin' the place into shape, and this year it looks like we'll have good crops of corn and barley . . . some wheat."

"Does Lance live far from you?"

"Him? A few miles. He's right neighborly when it comes to helpin' with raisin' barns an' such, but he keeps to hisself. I say it ain't right, a young man like him, but he just smiles at me and says I shouldn't worry, but I do. He ought to have hisself a woman."

"What's it like? His place, I mean."

"Comfortable. Squared logs that fit snug, windows all around, and a puncheon floor in the bedroom, stone-flag floors else-where. He done nigh all of it hisself, sleeping under a tree until he had it built.

"He split his own shakes, an' taken time about it. I expect he was most of six months at that house. He rarely goes to town. I couldn't figure that out. None of us could, until we found out he was Kilkenny.

"Seems like he likes bein' by hisself, although he's always ready to he'p anybody in need. He's a good hunter. Keeps hisself in fresh meat all the while, an' he wanders a good bit. He's got hisself a good vegetable garden but he gets much of what he needs from the forest. I lived around Injuns all my life but never knowed one who knew as much about livin' off the country as him."

When darkness fell, Jaime Brigo came to the door. "It is time," he said, "they are eating now."

"Enjoyed it, ma'am. Hope you'll come up an' set with me sometime. It's been a spell since I talked to ary city woman."

She mounted, and riding beside Brigo, rode slowly away.

Nita Riordan returned to her sitting room, then after a sip or two of tea she walked across to her desk and picked up a speaking tube that led to the bar.

"Sam? Ask Price Dixon to come in."

It was only a moment until there was a tap at the door, and then the gambler entered. "Price? Do you know Trent?"

"I know him. He's a good man."

"Did you know he was Lance Kilkenny?"

"I am not surprised." Price Dixon never revealed how much he knew, and always knew more than suspected.

"You saw him fight King Bill?"

Dixon smiled. "It was a rare treat. I never saw a more com-plete whipping given to anyone, although Hale is a tough man."

"How do you think Kilkenny would do with Turner?"

"With *Turner?* Tombull? Why, I never thought of such a thing, to tell you the truth. Tombull Turner is a pro, a very experienced fighter, and a tough one."

"Lance wants to fight him."

"*Wants* to? He's crazy! I can't imagine anybody wanting to fight Turner. Why, in God's world?"

"He thinks it is the only chance they will get to offer their side of things to Halloran. He thinks he'll get a chance to speak to him from the ring, and that Hale won't dare stop him."

"That makes a kind of sense, but there should be an easier way. Kilkenny and Turner?" He thought about that. "Dammit, Nita, but I'd like to see it. I really would! What a scrap that would be!

"You know," he exclaimed suddenly, "Kilkenny might have a chance, at that. He's good. I noticed the way he moved in that Hale fight. He's boxed some, knows his way around a ring, I'd say.

"Hale had help, you know. Kilkenny was kicked several times when he was down, tripped at least once. He hits very fast, and he's accurate.

"But Turner? The man's good, Nita. He's very good indeed."

"And he's fighting Sandoval."

Price looked around at her. He had walked to the sideboard and was pouring himself a drink. "Do you *want* Kilkenny to fight Turner?"

"No. I certainly do not." She smiled. "He's my man, Price, come what may. He is the only man I ever wanted, and I followed him here. Shameless of me, wasn't it? But I know he wants me too, and it is just his misguided sense of chivalry that keeps us apart. He doesn't want me to be a widow."

"I understand. In his place I'd feel the same. You have to face it, Nita, Kilkenny is a gunfighter with a reputation. There's no way he can escape it.

"I've seen him in action, and he is quick, unbelievably quick. What is more, he's accurate and he's cool. It is one thing, you know, to shoot at a target, another thing when the target is shooting back at you. Many a man who was supposed to be very fast suddenly blows up when he realizes *he* can be killed."

"You asked if I wanted Lance to fight Turner, and I said I did not. That's true. But Lance wants to fight him, and to me that comes first."

Price tasted his drink. "Nita, you and I know that anything can be done. If the fight is arranged and Sandoval doesn't get here, then the only man around who could make it interesting for Turner is Kilkenny . . . Trent, if you will."

"Could you keep Sandoval from getting here? I wouldn't want him hurt."

"I know that, and, yes, I could keep him from it. You know, he's only getting two hundred for the fight. If he wins, a bit more. But he isn't going to win, and I am sure he knows it.

"I also know that Rosa McNeil, a girl he's excited about, just came into the country. She's stopping in Mountain City for a few days. If somebody got two hundred dollars to Sandoval and the word that Rosa was in Mountain City, he could forget all about that fight."

"Then do it. I may be foolish. I may get Lance hurt, but what he wants I want for him. And I do know that Tom Halloran loves a fighter. He's as Irish as Kilkenny is, and he's been a follower of the prizefighting business all his life, as a spectator and enthusiast."

"It will be done." Price smiled. "Nita, you're quite a woman. You must remember, though, that Lance may not have that classic profile any longer when the fight is over."

She shrugged. "I am not in love with a profile, Price. I am in love with a man."

TWELVE

They loaded four kegs of water on the wagon and they each took a canteen. They took shovels, rope, and a long pole for a lever. With Bartram on the driver's seat, they started out.

Kilkenny, riding the buckskin again, led the way through the newly cut gap in the trees and down the steep slope. They tied a heavy log to the back of the wagon to keep it from running up on the heels of the mules. Cautiously they started down.

It was slow, painstaking travel. A dozen times Kilkenny dismounted to roll a stone from the road, yet at last they came to the bottom. Quince cut loose the log they had dragged for a brake.

The air was still and hot. It was a bleak, broken land with little vegetation. "Let's roll 'em!" Kilkenny said.

Before leaving the cliff he had taken a sight on a distant peak that he knew to be in the area of Blazer, but knowing the dust storms to be bad, he had brought along a compass. He had taken a sight on the distant peak and now he rechecked. The smoky haze that often hung over the area made outlines vague, but the trail they were following led roughly westward. How closely the trail would hold to the course he had set, he did not know, or even how long the road would be visible.

The slightest touch of wind stirred the fine dust into the air, and their horses' hooves and the wagon added to it. Slowly they moved westward. Twice they had to turn aside from great drifts of dust that reached across their path. Here and there Kilkenny found it easier to walk along and lead the buckskin, as there were obstacles to be moved from the trail. There was very little growth.

When they had been traveling what his watch told him was an hour, he held up a hand. They stopped and bunched around the wagon. With a damp piece of sacking brought for the purpose, the men sponged out the nostrils of the horses.

Jack Moffit had insisted on coming along with the wagon. He stood up on the seat, looking all about. "Where are we now?" he asked.

Nobody replied, and after a minute he said, "How far have we come?"

"Maybe three miles," Quince said. "Might be less."

Even though they carried no load but the kegs of water and the tools, the wagon was heavy, for the dust was rarely less than six inches deep and often they pulled through drifts that were as much as two feet in depth.

After a few minutes Kilkenny mounted again, and once more they pushed on. Before them, something large and dark loomed through the dust. It was a long, low, basaltic cliff that might have been a flow of lava. Kilkenny knew little of such things, except a few words picked up here and there from surveyors or when working in the mines.

The trail turned south, and after something over a half-mile it rounded the end of the obstruction and headed back north again, but northwest, actually. Twice they descended into deep water courses and climbed out of them. The tracks were all old. They saw little vegetation and no tracks of animals, not even of snakes or lizards.

At the end of the second hour they paused again. This time in the shade of a low cliff. There was no talking. The heat was intense and all were tired. Kilkenny offered no comment, but he was sure they had made no more than two miles, if as far.

Rising, he walked out from the shelter of the rock and climbed to a better position. There was a haze that seemed mostly heat waves now, but he could see little. Here and there a roll of the land, a butte, or some rocks. It was unbelievably dry, yet far ahead he could see what looked like a line drawn across in front of them. His glasses told him no more than his eyes because of the heat waves.

They started on. The sand was deep, their progress slow. Time and again they turned from the trail to find an easier way, then came back to the trail after circling some obstacle.

Quince came alongside. "Be glad when it's sundown," he said.

Kilkenny nodded. "Something up ahead. Can't quite make it out. A low wall maybe, sort of dike."

"I seen 'em. Outcrops that run for miles sometimes, but mostly only a few yards."

Kilkenny glanced at the mules pulling the wagon. They would have to rest more often, as the mules were breathing heavily. And they were pulling an almost empty wagon.

Suddenly the buckskin stopped. Before them was a wide, almost unbroken expanse of white marred by no black outcroppings of rock. He urged the horse on, but the buckskin refused to move.

Quince rode up. "What's the matter?"

"Don't know. Buck just stopped all of a sudden." He swung down and started forward and felt the earth suddenly turn to jelly under his feet. He cried out and tried to leap backward, but his feet were caught. Luckily he had hold of the bridle reins. He took a turn around his wrist. "Back up, Buck! Back!"

The horse backed up and pulled him free. Quince helped him to his feet. "Quicksand," he said, "or something like it. Must be springs under there."

"There's water under all this southern part of the territory," Kilkenny said, "and some of the biggest caves in the world, most of them never even seen by men. Most of the rivers run underground, and some of them in mighty deep canyons."

The thought stopped him. That old Indian had said something about canyons.

The wagon drew up behind them, with Saul and Jackie Moffit. "You sit tight," Kilkenny said. "I'll try to find a way around."

"And I'll go the other way," Quince offered.

Kilkenny turned the buckskin and let him have his head. The horse was no more anxious than he to get caught in quicksand, and would be likely to find a way around. A mountain-bred mustang like this one was almost as sagacious as a mule about such things.

Yet when he had ridden for some distance, well over a mile, the quicksand seemed to be curving around toward him, and he turned the horse and rode back.

Quince was waiting. "Just a few hundred yards yonder. There's higher ground. She's rocky but passable."

"Good." He let Quince lead off, and he followed the wagon. What he had called quicksand might be an alkali sink, and might not be deep, yet certainly too deep to cross.

Hour after hour they struggled on. It looked like a dry camp tonight. Weariness made his limbs leaden, and he knew the others were no better off. His sweat-soaked shirt had taken on so much of the white dust that now that it was drying it was very like cement. They stopped oftener now, and twice more they had sponged out the nostrils of the horses and mules and had given each of them a little water from a rag, squeezed into their mouths.

The trail led into acres and acres of black outcroppings of an old lava flow, crumbled and broken and drifted with dust and sand. Time had ceased to matter, and they lived only for the brief stops and their dreams of the coolness of the night before them.

Kilkenny was no longer sure of the compass. Mineral out-croppings might disturb it, and he was hard put to check their various weavings and turnings.

They lost the trail. It suddenly vanished on hard-packed sand and gravel, undoubtedly all evidence of it having blown away long since. Kilkenny drew up and waited for Quince.

"They were pointed that way"—he gestured—"so I guess we'd better keep going until we see some reason to change direction."

He pushed on, and the sun slowly died behind the western mountains and the cool evening came, and Quince came up to him again. "The mules are done in, Kilkenny. We've got to stop."

"I know. I've been looking for a place. You know, they camped somewhere, those other people did. I've been watching for a campfire site, charcoal maybe, or a circle of stones."

"We'd better stop."

"Just a little farther."

Kilkenny started on, and he heard the wagon creak in protest as it started after him, and then just fifty yards farther along he found it.

The ground broke sharply off, and the road turned hard right and went down on an easy grade. There was a good four acres of ground shielded by cliffs all around, except where an ancient stream had entered, then left. The stream had long since dried up, but there was a seep of water from the rock, and a shallow pool of only a few inches' depth and a few feet in diameter at the base.

He led the way down. Black basaltic cliffs around, nowhere more than fourteen or fifteen feet high, and there were the charred rocks of an old fire circle, a few bits of charcoal not quite covered by the white dust. Piled in a corner of the wall away from any possible rain was a small stack of firewood.

"They brought that with them," Bartram commented. "There's not a tree within miles."

"When we come back," Kilkenny said, "we'll bring some and drop it off."

They stripped the harness from the mules and let them roll, then took them to water. Kilkenny tasted it. "All right," he said, "a mite brackish."

Bartram took the lid from one of the kegs. "I'll use what we brought for coffee."

Quince put a small fire together, and Bart put the pot on, then went to preparing supper. Quince stretched out on the ground, looking up at the stars.

Kilkenny took his Winchester. "Come on, Jack. We'll scout around."

The sun was gone, yet some light remained. Slowly they skirted the small hollow. Here and there the river that had once run through here had hollowed the walls until there was some overhang. It was not too dark to see tracks, but they saw none. It was a bleak and lonely place.

Under one of the overhangs they found some Indian writing. Kilkenny indicated it. "Very old," he said. "Maybe before the white man."

He looked around. "There's some water, there's shelter from the wind, and some shade. You can bet men and animals have been coming here for thousands of years."

"Can you read the signs?"

"Me? No . . . not really. Some of them I can figure out because they are like the sign language, like talking with the hands."

One symbol was a man's open hand with five fingers. "Could mean several things. Maybe he's just trying to show us that he, too, had a hand. That he could grasp, feel, touch."

"How long do you think it's been since anybody was across here?"

Kilkenny shrugged. "A big tree like that one we cut would take no less than seventy years to decay, and it could be much longer. Those younger trees were at least ten years old, but I'd think they were more. My guess is that somebody built this road or used it a few times somewhere back in the 1850's. Probably they found an Indian trail for starters."

At daybreak they started on once more, but the day began

with a gust of wind and a few spattering drops of rain. That was all the rain there was, but the wind continued and soon the air was filled with choking, blinding, clinging dust particles, and with it all, stifling heat. They lost all thought of food or family, thinking only of getting across, of escaping.

Kilkenny was no longer sure of the compass, but the buckskin plodded on as though guided by some mystic means known only to him. Dazed with heat and weariness, they moved on, blind to all but the longed-for end of their journey at some impossible distance ahead.

Kilkenny drew up, trying to peer through the blinding dust to see some landmark, something.

The buckskin tugged at the bit impatiently and then started on of his own volition, and Kilkenny let him go. They might be wandering in circles; his only hope was that he thought the horse was climbing a little, that the saddle was tilting under him. Abruptly the buckskin stopped, and he found himself staring at the black upthrust of a cliff. It loomed before them, black and sheer, yet at the base the dust seemed a little thinner.

The mules came up close. "Pull up here!" he yelled. "I'll scout along the face!"

Quince shook his head. "Better get some rest first, an' let your hoss have some. That was a rough pull."

Kilkenny swung down, and taking the piece of sacking, he began sponging out the nostrils of the horse, and then of the mules. Bartram did likewise.

Lifting a keg down, they led each horse to it, and then the mules. They emptied one keg, then another.

They rested a half-hour and then Kilkenny could wait no longer. He had never been able to stop short of a goal, and he could not now. "We're across," he said to Bartram. "Now we've got to get up on top."

Leaving the buckskin to rest, he walked along the face of the cliff, stepping over rocks and fallen trees. He had always had this something in him that kept driving him on, even when all good sense suggested he rest or wait. Yet now he had walked no more than three hundred yards when he saw what he was looking for. He stopped, unable to believe their good fortune. With all their weaving back and forth, they had succeeded in holding to the trail often enough to have brought them to where they wished to go. Before him a rough trail wound up the cliff face!

It was dusk when they reached the top of the road and pulled up under the pines. There they built a small fire, made coffee, and warmed some food. There was a small meadow close by, and there they hobbled the horses and mules and let them rest. There was a seep at the edge of the meadow with a trickle from a spring and a little standing water with some cattails growing at its edge.

Kilkenny drank the strong black coffee and it tasted good, but his lids grew heavy and he almost dropped the plate of food from his hand. He looked around, and Bartram was already stretched out and asleep without even taking the time to unroll his bed.

"I slept some in the wagon," Jack said. "You go to sleep. Come midnight, I'll wake you up."

He slept like he was drugged until Quince shook him awake. "The boy woke me up," he said, "but you'd better take over now."

Refreshed, he went to the blackened pot and filled his cup. The night was still except for the subdued snores of Bartram. A wind rustled leaves on an aspen not far off. The wind had blown the dust away, and the clouds as well. The sky was clear and spangled with stars. Walking to the seep, he stripped off his shirt and washed the dust from his face, body, and hair. He shook out the shirt and put it back on, drank deep at the spring, then walked back to the fire.

He listened. It was very still out there. Hitching a six-shooter into position just in case, he proceeded to wipe the Winchester clean and then he ran a ramrod down the barrel. Then one by one he cleaned his six-shooters.

In the darkness, thoughts came easily and he sat near the fire but back from it a little to observe the shadows better, and his thoughts considered the situation at Cedar.

If he could get the fight with Tombull Turner, he would have a chance to speak to Halloran. There would be others there, but he had a very special reason for talking to Halloran, and if he was not mistaken, a very special reason for claiming his attention, and perhaps his sympathy as well.

He would be going into the fight as an underdog, which gave him a little edge on their sympathy. He was also the smaller man, and he was the unknown amateur against a professional of proven ability. Kilkenny was perfectly aware that he could expect a beating. On the other hand, few men were in better shape than he was, and he was sure he could last long enough to make an impression.

The fight would, of course, as were all fights under the London prize-ring rules, be a fight to the finish. A knockdown was the end of a round, which might mean only a second or two or might mean nine or ten minutes or longer. A slip could mean the end of a round if a man fell, or one or the other could be thrown, for much was legal under the bare-knuckle rules. Kilkenny had seen a fighter get a headlock on another and then pound his face with the free hand for several minutes.

King Bill would certainly have his guests in ringside seats, which would put them close to the ropes and in a good position to talk. Time would be the thing, and the choice of the right moment. Hale would be expecting a quick victory, and Turner as well.

Coldly Kilkenny appraised himself. Like all fighting men, he had confidence in his own ability. He had fought many times in the rough-and-tumble scraps of the frontier, and even as a boy he had fought a good deal at school. During the days when he lived in the East he had learned boxing from Jem Mace, onetime heavyweight champion of the world, and one of the cleverest of the old-time fighters. Mace was an English gypsy fighter who boxed much on this side of the pond. He was a shrewd and clever man who used his head for something other than a parking place for a couple of ears.

King Bill did not know that Kilkenny had ever boxed. No doubt their fight had given him some inkling, but not enough. Years of rugged life in the open had also given him hard physical condition and superb strength as well as staying quality.

These were considerable assets, but he had something else that was just as important. He had seen Turner fight. This could make the difference, for Turner knew nothing of him.

Yet in all honesty he could hope for little more than to make a game fight of it and win some sympathy and at least a friendly hearing.

When he returned to the Cup he would soak his hands in brine, and he would plan to wear driving gloves in the ring. They not only protected the fists, but they would cut like a knife. Some of the younger fighters had been doing just that, and he had tried it and liked the feel of them.

Now there was no sound but that of the forest. Dawn was not too far off. He added a little fuel to the small fire and poured another cup of coffee. Sitting with it, he slowly and methodically went over in his mind every move he had seen Turner make.

When dawn came he slept for a half-hour or so and felt fresh and ready. Quince had finished breakfast and they sat together.

"Quince," he said, "you know Blazer. What do you think about it?"

Hatfield shrugged. "Reckon they won't be expectin' us to come from here. I been givin' it thought, and it seems to me we'll come into town from the far side, so we got a good chance of gettin' right into town before they know we're there."

"Good!" Kilkenny turned to Bartram. "You know the team. Stay by the wagon and keep your gun handy. At the first shot, we'll come to you.

"Saul, you an' Jack hustle the grub to the wagon, and Quince will stand by to cover you."

"How about you?" Bart asked.

"I'll make the deal for the supplies and then I'll nose around to see what I can find out about the other wagon. Lije and the rest may be all right, but I want to be sure."

Mounting up, they started out. The road they followed showed no evidence of travel, and soon they discovered why. It had long since been fenced off. They took down the bars of the worm fence and drove through into a well-used road. Kilkenny waited and replaced the bars, although he did not rebind them with rawhide.

There was very little to the town. Two rows of ramshackle saloons and a store faced each other across the street. The usual assortment of town loafers sat on benches before the Crossroads and the Temple of Chance. Two cow ponies stood three-legged in front of the Wagon Wheel.

Lance Kilkenny took the thongs from his six-guns. He wanted no trouble, but this was a hard town, and there were men here who even if they knew he was Kilkenny wouldn't care. Names and reputations meant little to the average western man, and for every gunfighter with a reputation there were four just as good whom nobody had ever heard of. And they liked it that way.

THIRTEEN

Lance Kilkenny rode past Perkins' General Store and dismounted in front of the Wagon Wheel. Bartram pulled up parallel to the walk in front of the store and began to fill his pipe, his rifle beside him.

Saul and Jack walked into the store, and Quince leaned against a corner of the store building and bit off a chew of tobacco. His rifle was in the hollow of his arm and he wore a huge Walker Colt.

A rider turned into the street and swung down in front of the Wagon Wheel not far from Kilkenny. The rider glanced at him briefly, then went inside. The man was big, with red hair and a beard.

Quince crossed the walk to Kilkenny. "That gent who just came in was wearin' an ivory-handled Colt with a chipped ivory on the right side." His narrow face was cold, his expression bitter. "That's Jody Miller's gun he was packin'."

"Jody was with the first wagon," Kilkenny said.

"He surely was," Quince said. "I reckon I'd better put him to the question."

"Wait, Quince. I'm going in there. You keep your eyes open, but remember, we need grub first of all. Everything comes second to that. Meantime, maybe I can find out something."

Kilkenny was a man without illusions. The chance that there might be two such guns in such an area at the same time was beyond reason, and knowing Jody Miller, he also knew that if the red-haired man had Jody's gun, he had taken it from his body.

Kilkenny walked over to the Wagon Wheel and went inside. The red-bearded man was at the bar. Two men who might have been cowpunchers sat at a table with the bartender and another man in a black coat. This man was enormously tall and enormously fat. That, he decided, would be Soderman.

"Come on, Shorty!" the red-beard said irritably. "I want a drink!"

"Take it easy, Gaddis." Shorty was a short, thickset man with an unshaven face. "I'll be with you in a minute."

Kilkenny was in no hurry, and the situation did not look good. No two men could be so big and fat, so this had to be Soderman. That placed Soderman and Gaddis. The other two might be ordinary cowhands in for a drink and not hunting trouble. One of them might be Ratcliff, who was rated a dangerous man. Rye Pitkin was somewhere around, but Kilkenny did not see him. He knew Pitkin, and Pitkin knew him.

Judging by appearances, Shorty could be expected to back up whatever Soderman did. If that was Jody's gun, then the other wagon had been attacked and probably wiped out.

A slow rage began to build within him at the thought of those hard-working, honest men being ambushed by such as these. He was aware that Soderman was watching him, and the big man was a cool customer, very cool.

Shorty walked over behind the bar. "All right, Gaddis, what'll you have?"

"Rye," Gaddis said, and for the first time he really noticed Kilkenny, his glance sharpening as he noted the dusty clothes and the guns. Not many men wore two guns. He stared hard at Kilkenny, but Lance had his hat brim pulled low and seemed not to be aware.

"Make mine rye, too," Kilkenny suggested mildly. Then he turned his head to look at Soderman. "You drinkin'? Have one on me."

"Of course." The fat man got up and moved with an astonishing ease and lightness of foot. Kilkenny's attention sharpened. This man could move. "I always like to know who I'm drinkin' with, though."

"Not so where I come from," Kilkenny replied. "A drink's a drink."

"Of course." He stepped up to the bar, and Kilkenny moved aside in such a way that Soderman must step between Kilkenny and Gaddis. Soderman hesitated only an instant, then stepped up to the bar. "Not often you see a man packin' two guns," he added. "I thought every man who wore that kind of hardware knew Doc Soderman."

"I've heard the name." Kilkenny let his eyes drift to the table Soderman had left. One of the men was rolling a smoke, the other idly riffling a deck of cards. Either of them was in position to draw quickly. Red Gaddis had turned to face Kilkenny.

The whole setup looked a little too pat. Did they know he was from the high country. It was a tight situation, and he was going to have to relax them a little, to take a little steam off the top.

"Heard there might be a job up this way," he commented mildly, "and I could use a job where it's quiet."

"Away from the law?" Soderman suggested.

"Away from everything."

"We have law here. King Bill Hale is the law," Soderman said.

"Heard of him," Kilkenny said. "Heard he pays well."

"You hear a lot," Gaddis said. He was staring at Kilkenny, his eyes mean. He took another drink and continued to stare.

Kilkenny glanced at him from under the brim of his hat. "I make it my business to listen," he said quietly. "A man can learn a lot that way."

"Maybe you listen too much!" Gaddis said. He was in a truculent mood, and the whiskey was having its effect. Kilkenny's drink was on the bar, untouched.

"You want to show me how much?" he asked mildly. He was sure there would be no shooting just yet. Soderman was still not sure of him, and Gaddis didn't care. He was wondering if Soderman knew Quince Hatfield was outside the window with a rifle.

Gaddis stepped away from the bar. "Yes, I want—"

"Stop it!" Soderman ordered. "Gaddis, you keep on that way and you'll get yourself killed."

"Not by him," he said scornfully, but he quieted down. It was a clear demonstration of who was in command here.

Kilkenny thought that despite his belligerence Gaddis had welcomed the interruption. Gaddis, he believed, was a killer but not a gunfighter. The sort of man who might dry-gulch some men riding a wagon. And he wore a gun with a chipped handle.

"Your friend's kind of edgy," Kilkenny commented.

"Forget it. He just likes to fight, that's all." He glanced at Kilkenny again. "You mentioned looking for work. There might just be a chance."

"Either that or I drift on through," Kilkenny said. He glanced pointedly at Gaddis' gun. "Seems you should be somebody I know," he said, "but I don't place the face. I never was much good on faces, anyway, but I always remember a man by his gun."

He tasted his whiskey, then put the glass back on the bar. "Every gun has its own special look, or maybe it's the way a man wears it. Take that one, now, with the chipped ivory butt. Nobody could forget a gun like that."

Gaddis was suddenly wary. His eyes went to Soderman, then back to Kilkenny. Before he could speak, Soderman looked straight into Kilkenny's eyes. "And where did you see that gun?"

"I was down to the capital," he said, "and saw that gun hangin' on a man named Jody Miller. He was comin' west to farm."

He wanted to worry Soderman, who was a cautious man. He wanted to plant a little seed of doubt.

"Miller stopped off in the capital to see some relatives and friends. Seems this Jody Miller didn't have much himself, but he was a well-thought-of man with a lot of relatives in important places who thought a lot of Jody. When I first noticed the gun, he was sitting at a table with Halloran and Wallace."

He had all of Soderman's attention now. The big man was worried, really disturbed. "This Miller knew Halloran and Wallace?"

"Oh, he knew them, all right! They were talking friendly-like, and as they mentioned this part of the country, I paid attention, as I was planning to ride this way, even then. It seems Miller had stopped off to visit these people. He had known Wallace for some time, but Halloran was married to Jody's sister. I heard Halloran say he was going to come out and pay Jody a visit after he was settled."

Kilkenny tasted his whiskey again. "I think Miller was in town to file his homestead on some place up in the mountains near here."

Kilkenny glanced at Gaddis, his face expressionless. "I expect you'll be mighty glad to see them, Miller. It's surely nice to have a big official like that for a friend."

Lance could have laughed at Gaddis had he not been filled with bitterness at the thought of their wagon waylaid and their friends killed.

Gaddis had actually been called by name only a few minutes before, but Kilkenny acted as if he had not heard. The man was obviously worried, and not by Kilkenny, of whom he knew nothing. Was it Soderman? Or Hale? Or simply that he had been caught red-handed in a murder? Or at least an ambush.

"Odd," Kilkenny continued, "you've got red hair. I'd have sworn Miller had black hair. I—"

"It was yel . . ." Gaddis started to interrupt, then realized what he had said.

"Yellow," Kilkenny agreed. "That's right. He was a blond. I couldn't remember that, but you did, and you're packin' Miller's gun. Now, how do you explain that?"

Suddenly a door behind Kilkenny opened. He felt the flesh tighten along the back of his neck. He dared not turn. He had been deliberately baiting them, hoping for more information. Now, suddenly, he was boxed in.

Soderman seemed to make up his mind, or perhaps he had been stalling, waiting for this to happen. Assurance returned to him and he said, "Why, howdy, Rye! You should come over and meet our friend here! Says he recognizes the gun Red's a-wearin'."

Rye Pitkin walked around to where he could see Kilkenny, and his face went stiff with shock. "You!" he said hoarsely. "Why . . ."

"Long way from the Pecos, isn't it, Rye? And from the Brazos, too. Now, Pitkin, you listen, and listen close. I'm not anxious to start shooting, but at least two of you are going to die, and I'm betting on three. You and Soderman will come first.

"My friends outside the windows will take care of Gaddis or anybody else who lifts a hand. Right now I am walking out of here, and you'd better impress it on your friends that starting some action won't do them any good."

Kilkenny backed toward the door. Soderman's eyes were hot with expectation mingled with some doubt. Why was Pitkin so obviously frightened? Who *was* this man?

Red Gaddis had turned slightly, watching Kilkenny. Rye read what was in his mind. "Red! For God's sake, don't! That's *Kilkenny!*"

Gaddis' hand came away from his gun as if suddenly burned. Warily he began to back off, as if distance could help.

Glass tinkled, and a long Kentucky rifle barrel slid into the room. "Now, if you're going to play it smart," Quince remarked, "you gents just hole up here an' get drunk, because the first one who makes a wrong move or sticks his head out is going to be dead."

The wagon was loaded. Bart sat on the wagon seat, reins in his hand, rifle across his knees. Jack Moffit sat beside him with his rifle in his two hands.

Saul was across the street, holding all their horses.

"Start the wagon, Bart. Take the Cedar trail. Jack, you stay with Bart, and be ready for trouble."

He crossed the street, swung aboard the buckskin, and slid his Winchester from the boot. The wagon moved out at a fast trot, he and the Hatfields following.

All three were looking back over their shoulders, so Lance saw what happened when Red Gaddis stepped into the street with a rifle in his hand. Quince half-turned his horse, and the rifle came up. He fired an instant before Gaddis, and the red-headed man took two quick steps into the street and fell, half his head blown away.

"He won't take no more guns off'n nobody!" Quince said.

There was a scattering of shots, and Kilkenny pulled up behind a log barn on the edge of town and swung down. "We're going to have to come back here, so we might as well let them know what the score is."

He saw a man start from the back of the Wagon Wheel and snapped a quick shot. The man stumbled and fell. Saul went down the street at a dead run, firing with his pistol. There was a smashing of window glass, and a man fell half out of a second-story window and lay sprawled across the sill.

Saul came back, shooting again and at a dead run.

At every movement, one of them fired.

"You boys cover me," Kilkenny said, "when I come back."

Leaving his horse, he sprinted down along the back of the buildings toward the Wagon Wheel.

He wanted Pitkin or Ratcliff, because he needed to know what had happened back there on the trail. Some or all of his friends might be dead, but he intended to find out. If they were dead, he could at least help to bury them, and maybe some of Hale's riff-raff along with them.

He drew up. The rear door of the saloon stood open. A man lay sprawled a few feet away from it, gun near his hand. He was dead.

FOURTEEN

Kilkenny stood behind the next building and waited, watching. He wanted Pitkin or Ratcliff under his gun. It was information he needed, and he would get nothing from Soderman unless the fat man decided of his own free will.

Several old boards lay on the ground behind the saloon, dry and parched from long exposure to sun and wind. On a sudden inspiration he holstered his gun, gathered several of the boards, some dry grass and smaller sticks, and lit a fire.

It was a little away from the buildings, but he hoped the smoke would blow into the saloon. He wanted them to think he was burning them out, which was the last thing he wished, as they needed the town as a supply base, and Perkins had sold them what they wanted without question.

As the boards caught fire, he stepped near the door of the saloon but well out of sight. The flames leaped up and the fire crackled. He added greener grass to the flames, and the wind carried the smoke through the open door.

A startled exclamation from within, and then a man rushed out and began kicking the boards away from the fire.

"All right!" Kilkenny spoke just loud enough for him to hear. "Don't move!"

It was Ratcliff, and the man stood like a statue, "What's the trouble, Kilkenny?" he said. "I never done nothing to you!"

"Turn around slowly, walk this way, and watch your hands."

Ratcliff was a weasel-faced man with shifty eyes and a slim, nervous body. He started moving but threw a quick glance at the open door. When he was within five feet, Kilkenny stopped him.

"All right, now, I want to know what happened to that other wagon. I want it fast and I want it clear-cut."

Ratcliff sneered. "You think I'd tell you? Go out there and

find out if you like. You'll be gettin' the same before you're home."

With one quick step Kilkenny grabbed the man by the shirt collar and slammed him against the side of the building. "You want a pistol-whipping? You're begging for it right now. Now, you start talking, and talk fast. I haven't the time to fool around."

"All right, all right!" Ratcliff said. "Leave me be. Won't do you any good, anyway, as you're not gettin' home. That other wagon loaded with grub, an' we let 'em get out of town. Then Soderman and about six men ambushed them."

"How many were killed?"

"We lost a man. We killed Miller and Wilson with the first volley. It was a Hatfield got our man, nailed him dead center."

"What happened to Hatfield and Hight?"

"Hight went down. I seen him fall. He was shot two or three times. We got Hatfield, too. Winged him, anyway. Hatfield got up an' dragged Hight into the rocks. We couldn't get to 'em."

"Then what?"

A voice roared from the saloon. It was Soderman. "Ratcliff! What in time are y' doin' out there?"

"Answer me. Then what?"

"Soderman said it would serve 'em right. He left them there to die, with two men to see they didn't get out of those rocks. They've had 'em pinned in there for two days now, an' no water."

"On the Blazer trail?"

"Almost to the turnoff to the peaks. Hell, they're dead by now. Ain't a damn thing you can do, Kilkenny, not even you."

With a swift move Kilkenny flipped Ratcliff's six-shooter from its holster. "All right," he said, "get going!"

Ratcliff lunged for the saloon door just as Soderman's huge bulk stepped into it. Soderman glimpsed Kilkenny and with a swift motion the fat man palmed his gun and fired. He was not a good hip shot, and his gun went off before it came level, dropping Ratcliff in his tracks.

Standing in the open, legs wide apart, Kilkenny fired as he drew. The bullet caught Soderman right in the center of that vast belly.

Soderman's face showed shock, and then fear as he realized he had been gut-shot. He started to lift his pistol again, but his knees buckled and he fell facedown on the steps. The pistol slipped from fingers that had lost their life and rattled on the boards below.

Kilkenny stepped over the big body and into the saloon. Rye Pitkin and Shorty were crouched by the front windows with rifles.

"Drop 'em!" he ordered. "Unbuckle your gun belts and let them fall. Now, step back away from them."

Surprised and helpless, the two men did as they were told. "Rye," Kilkenny said, "I've given you a break before, and now I'll do it again. The same goes for Shorty. You two mount and ride. If I ever see either of you around here again, I'll kill you on sight. I'll be coming back to Blazer, so be damned sure you aren't here!"

He scooped up the guns and backed toward the door. Then he ran to where the Hatfields waited. "Let's go!" he said. "Lije may still be alive!"

"You can handle the wagon," Quince said. "Me an' Saul, we'll get on down the trail."

"Go," Kilkenny told them, "and luck to you."

Bartram's relief was plain when Kilkenny came into sight. "Get rolling," Lance said. "We've a long way to go."

"What happened?"

"We won another round," Kilkenny explained, "and I doubt if we'll have any trouble in Blazer again."

"Perkins was all right," Bart said. "He just laid out what we asked for, and when we had it all, he wished us luck. He's a decent man."

Dust devils danced upon the desert's face, and the wagon, heavily loaded now, rumbled along slowly, bumping over stones in the roadway. Jack Moffit had tied his horse behind the wagon, and now he climbed into the saddle again to ride with Kilkenny.

This route skirted the desert wilderness they had crossed coming over, and was a much easier route, although a more dangerous one now. Only the fact that Lije was holed up back along the trail kept Kilkenny to it.

Rugged mountains rose up on their left, but on the right the timber thinned out and the pines gave way to cedar and then to the scattered sagebrush as it neared the desert's edge. There were frequent clumps of boulders, each one of which Kilkenny studied with care, although he expected no trouble yet.

Jack rode beside him, and Kilkenny knew the boy was eager to ask him about what happened in the settlement. He was just as loath to speak of it, but decided to satisfy the youngster's curiosity. After all, Jack was playing a man's part and deserved a man's share in all of it.

"Trouble back there, Jack. Some men were killed back there."

"Who was it? Did you kill 'em?"

"I killed one man . . . Soderman. I had to, Jack. He was one of the worst of them, and he had a gun in his hand and was shooting at me . . . or starting to. He killed one of his own men shooting at me.

"I wanted to know what happened to the other wagon. They might have had some of them as prisoners in the town, but Ratcliff said Lije was holed up down the trail, that they had killed Miller and Wilson."

"Gosh! Jody Miller! I *liked* him! I didn't know Mr. Wilson so much, but Jody was nice. He used to come by and see us. He was some kin to Ma . . . away back."

They rode for a while; then: "What about the others?"

"I let them go, Jack. I told Pitkin and Shorty to get out of the country. I think they'll go."

"We asked about the other wagon when we were in the store. They said they had loaded them with whatever they asked for. Perkins said nobody was going to tell him who to sell to. He had him a shotgun right alongside him all the time, and his wife had another."

Occasionally they paused to rest the mules. It was very hot. Kilkenny kept listening for shots, but the distance would be too great. He worried about the boys riding into an ambush in their hurry to get there, but then he reflected the Hatfields were too shrewd for that. Yet they would be eager to get there.

The road was longer, but there was no dust like there had been in the desert. Again and again Kilkenny's thoughts reverted to Nita. Would she marry Hale? He doubted it, and yet the man was a commanding figure, a not unhandsome man, and one of importance. He certainly had more to offer than a drifting gunfighter who would wind up someday facedown in a dusty street.

Of course, a few men had been able to leave it all behind and establish themselves as peaceful members of a community. He could always go east, but what would he do there? His adult life had been spent in the West, and in the East he would have no source of income. He had at times been a gambler, and had done well, but it was not a profession on which to build a life.

He drew rein and waited for the wagon to catch up. His eyes strayed down their back trail but saw nothing, and the road before them was so winding that they could see but a short distance.

"Bart," he warned, "it's still a few miles, but look alive. We may run into trouble."

"I haven't heard any shooting."

"Nor I, but we'd better be ready for trouble."

What could they have found? Was Lije dead? What of Jackson Hight? How many more must die before all of this was settled? Why should one land-hungry man push this fight upon peaceful men who wanted only to till their fields in peace?

It was a fair land, even at its worst, a good land in which men could grow and raise their families, but if fight they must, then they would fight with every lawful means.

Heat waves danced in the distance, a shimmering veil across the road before them. The tracks of the wagon were there, and some hoof prints superimposed upon them. His eyes strayed across the cedar-dotted hills and up through the boulders. Cicadas sang in the brush along the road until their sound became almost the voice of the wastelands.

Darkness came before they reached the site of the ambush. It could be only a few miles farther, but the mules were tired. Kilkenny waited for Bart to come up and then gestured into the cedars at one side of the road. It was a nest of boulders and cedars overlooking a small grassy meadow.

"We'd best camp," he said. "We don't want to go it blind."

They found a hollow among the rocks and made a small masked fire. There they made coffee and a hurried supper before putting out the fire. Coyotes began to sing at the stars before they were bedded down, and Kilkenny turned to Jack. "How about the first watch, Moffit?"

Bart looked around sharply but said nothing. That he was not sure of the boy's ability to stay awake and alert, Kilkenny could guess, but he knew Jack would try hard, and perhaps be more alert than an older man.

"Pay attention to the mules and horses, Jack. If they hear anything, they will show it. I'm going to keep Buck up close to camp, and he's better than a watchdog. When you've had a couple of hours of it, you wake up Bart. I'll take the last watch in the morning. Tell Bart to wake me up at two or so, if there's no trouble before."

It was a quiet night. When Bartram touched him, he was awake instantly, and tugging on his boots, he stood up, stamped his feet to settle them in place, and took his rifle and moved out.

"All peaceful," Bart said. "There's coyotes around, and I think there was a cat out there somewhere. Your buckskin acted up a little, snorting some, ears pricked. He didn't seem to pay the coyotes much mind."

"He doesn't," Lance replied. "He'll take right after a coyote. A lion's a different thing. He's right wary of them. Coming across a pass one time in the Absorokas, one jumped us, lit right on Buck's hindquarters, and you never saw such pitching in your life. The lion evidently was a big young one, and he jumped before he was sure of what he saw . . . figured Buck was a deer or something. Probably only a glimpse."

"What happened?"

"He pitched some, like I said, got a few nasty scratches, and the lion took off into the brush. He was probably more scared than we were."

Bartram went to his blankets, and Kilkenny moved out from the others to where he was away from the small sounds of their turnings and mutterings and breathing. He moved about a little, talking to the horses. The mules were feeding, and after a while they dozed and their very complacency told him he had nothing to worry about.

At dawn they had a quick breakfast of bacon and cold cornbread and pushed on. Now the hills came closer, the sides steeper. There was no breeze.

The mules leaned into the harness as the grade stiffened. They heard a rider coming before they saw him, and Kilkenny shucked his Winchester. Jack Moffit took the reins from Bartram, and Bart settled down behind some of the barrels and boxes with his rifle ready. Kilkenny recognized the rider as soon as he came within sight. It was Saul.

"Found 'em," Saul explained briefly when he rode up. "Both are alive. Mighty bad off, though. Hight was shot several times, and there's three bullets hit Lije. They was holed up in the rocks, more dead than alive."

When they reached the cluster of rocks, they pulled the wagon in close. The other wagon was there, and only one mule was dead. Another had a long scratch from a bullet, but aside from being nervous over the flies, it seemed healthy enough. Quince had the two men laid out in the shade.

Hight's wounds showed signs of care. Wounded as he was, Lije had found time to care for Hight, to wash his wounds and put makeshift bandages on him from material in the wagon. His lips seemed moist, and he evidently had not lacked for water.

Lije they had found near him, propped against a boulder with three rifles laid around him and four six-shooters. He had Hight's guns and evidently those of one of the men who had been killed. He was forted up and ready for a fight, although obviously in bad shape.

Lije was in bad shape for water. Obviously he had been giving most of what little they had to Jackson Hight.

They made a place for the two men in the wagon and lifted them gently in. A blanket was placed across two barrels as an awning to keep the sun off them.

"Jack," Kilkenny suggested, "you drive their wagon. That will leave Quince, Saul, and me to ride escort."

While he and Bartram prepared the places for the two wounded men, Saul and Quince buried Miller and Wilson in shallow graves. Later they would come back and recover the bodies, but there was no time now. They might be attacked at any moment.

Saul rode ahead, and the two wagons pulled back into the road. Quince came up alongside of him. His face was grim. "If Lije dies," he said, "we uns will be huntin' scalps.

"We lost Hatfield blood all the way west. Pa's half-brother was kilt down Texas way, fightin' for independence. His own blood brother was killed by the Santee Sioux in Dakota, an' Ma lost a sister and her children on the Kansas plains. Wherever we lost blood, we taken blood."

"Maybe we can get this settled without that, Quince. The old days and ways are passing out."

"You show me the way, Kilkenny. You show me how to reason with the likes of Hale, Soderman, and them."

"Soderman is dead, Quince. So is Gaddis. Both of them were in on the attack. Ratcliff is dead, too. They've been paying for it."

"Ain't no paying for a Hatfield," Quince replied stubbornly. "They fetched it to us. Now let them reap what they sowed.

Anyway, these are hired hands. Hale's the man behind it, and Hale and that Cub of his, they are the ones we want."

Kilkenny said no more, for Quince Hatfield's face was drawn in hard, bleak lines. He knew how the man felt. Once he would have felt the same.

Maybe he still did.

FIFTEEN

All was quiet in the Hatfield Cup when the little cavalcade rode in. The Hatfield women did not cry or carry on. They went about doing what had to be done.

Kilkenny looked around for Alice Miller. She stood at one side, twisting her apron in her hands, looking for Jody. Suddenly she turned and went inside. He waited for a minute and then went in.

"Ma'am," he said gently, "we buried him shallow. We will go get him soon. He was a good man, a mighty good man." He rested a hand on her shoulder and talked quietly and soothingly, yet there was nothing to be said, nothing to be done now—a good man was gone, leaving a wife and a small family.

When he went outside again, there was a cold, bitter anger within him. For a moment he looked at Buck, felt the weight of the guns at his hips, and remembered the contempt of Cub Hale, the arrogance of his father.

No . . . now was not the time. Jody was gone, and Wilson too, but what they had fought for must not be lost. The surest way to make Hale pay was not to kill him but to destroy him and what he had done, to win so the rest of them could keep their homes.

Parson Hatfield was shaking with anger. "That's two more, Kilkenny! I'm a-goin' to kill Bill Hale!"

"Wait, Parson. We've got to wait. Has there been any trouble here?"

"Smithers ain't come back."

"When did he leave?"

"Yesterday mornin'. Wasn't no holdin' him. He was worried about his place and his stock. He sets great store by that crop he's planted."

"He could be holed up somewhere." Kilkenny thought back over the country between. "He wasn't much of a woodsman, but he has good common sense. He might be smart enough to hide out."

He told Parson then of all that had transpired, of the bitter struggle to cross the wild country, of their arrival in Blazer and of Perkins' attitude, then of the fighting.

"We can cross that rough country anytime, unless the wind is blowing. Then it would be best just to hole up and wait it out. This time we pushed on through because of need, but we scouted the trail, and I think any of the boys who went with us could find the way across now.

"They can't bottle us up now unless they wipe out Perkins, which they might do, but he doesn't shape up like a man you could rub out very easy.

"If a man got caught in a sandstorm down in those bottoms, you'd probably never hear of him again, but that need not happen. Anyway," he added, "we have supplies enough for a while."

"I knowed that Gaddis, an' Soderman too. Never liked them, either one," Parson commented. "That Soderman, he was one of the worst."

"Parson," Kilkenny suggested, "now that we've shown it can be done, they might try to come at us that way. We have to keep it in mind."

"I hope they try it," Parson replied grimly. "I surely hope so!"

It was a long time before Kilkenny slept. He lay awake thinking of Tombull Turner. He slowly opened and closed his hands. The soreness had gone from them. They felt good. Suddenly he sat up, folding his arms around his knees. That Turner, now. Sure, he was big and he was tough and he was skilled, but he put his pants on one leg at a time like any other man.

The belly was the place, and the heart. What had Jem Mace told him? "Get 'em where they live, boy. Downstairs. I don't care how tough they are, get 'em in the belly and you'll slow 'em down."

Well, maybe. Just maybe.

After a while he lay on his back and looked up at the stars shining down through the pines. When he next turned over it was daybreak and the stars were gone. The smell of the pines was still there, and the smell of coffee and of bacon frying.

Yet when he looked toward the house, he saw Saul.

The tall, lanky boy was standing in the open, hands hanging

empty at his sides. He was just standing, staring. When he saw Kilkenny he said, "Lijah's dead. He died in the night, quiet-like. Sally was a-settin' up with him, an' Quince, he was awake."

"Dammit, Saul! I'm sorry. I . . ."

"He was just a-lyin' there," Quince said, coming from the house. "He just reached over and took my hand and said, 'Stay with 'em, boy!' an' he was gone. Just like that."

"There'll be blood on the moon now," Saul said grimly. "And it'll be Hale blood."

O'Hara came out to join them. "Last night," he said, "I rode all night goin' an' coming. I went to get that doc down to Cedar, but he set up a squawl. He wouldn't come no way. We sneaked into town to reach him, but he made such a fuss we were lucky to get away."

"We will remember that," Kilkenny said.

O'Hara shook his head regretfully. "Kilkenny, what if we don't win? They may just wipe us out entirely. Even if you talk to those men from the territorial capital, what can they do?"

"They can stop it, O'Hara. But don't worry. We are going to win."

"Supposing they won't listen? After all, Hale's entertaining them. He's a smart man, and he knows how to cater to people like that."

"If they do not listen, O'Hara, I promise you one thing. I'll go down to Cedar with my guns on and I won't come back as long as either one of them is alive.

"I've seen men die, and good men have died, and none of it need be, except for one man who has lost all perspective. Personally I believe it is Cub who is behind him, pushing him on.

"I'm sorry about them all. I'm sorry about Lije because even when badly hurt himself, he cared for Hight. He wasn't seventeen yet, but nobody was ever more of a man."

"When you ride down there, Kilkenny," Parson said, "I will ride with you."

"No, you stay here. What happens to me doesn't matter all that much, but you stay here so that no matter what happens, we will win in the end. I want your homes to stay in these high meadows, Parson, and it will take you or somebody like you to see that they do.

"As for me, it doesn't matter that much. Anybody who has

used a gun as much as I have is living on borrowed time anyway. If it doesn't come one place, it will come another.

"The dumb ones, they think they will live forever, that there's some charm that protects them. They never know better until they are down in the dust and dying. Whenever a gun becomes a way of life, its owner has condemned himself."

For several days all was quiet. Kilkenny chopped corn, helped repair some fences, cut wood for the fires, and generally kept busy. Several times he climbed to the top of a nearby peak that gave a good view of the trails. On two days he cut wood continuously, and as he worked he thought of Tombull Turner.

Mace had been a thinking fighter and he had taught Kilkenny well. He went over in his mind all that he remembered, how Turner held his hands, the way his feet moved when he advanced and retreated, how he liked to set himself before throwing a punch. He thought of how Turner threw a right or left and how he reacted when hit, how he blocked or tried to evade a punch.

Each fighter develops unconscious habits. A certain method of blocking or countering is easy for him, and so he uses it more often than not, even though he knows other methods. A good boxer, expecting a long fight, will feel out an opponent, testing his reactions to various blows and studying his methods. Then he will know what he must do.

Kilkenny knew that if he stayed with Turner long enough to get his chance to speak to Halloran it would be only because of brains, because he could think faster, better, and more effectively than Turner. He had the advantage of knowing much of him, while Turner knew nothing or next to nothing of him. Whatever he heard about the Hale fight would be largely ignored by Turner. Hale was not a professional, and the fight had been rough-and-tumble, with no skill apparent.

There was no news from Cedar. By now they evidently knew of what had taken place at Blazer.

On the third day after their return from Blazer, Saul rode in with a poster he had torn from a tree. It announced the fight between Turner and Sandoval, a fight to the finish, London prize-ring rules, for a purse of one thousand dollars in gold.

"For that much I'd fight him myself," Jesse commented.

"The trouble is," Bart said dryly, "you've got to win to collect. They fight winner-take-all."

"You mean the loser gets nothin'?"

"He gets a beating," Bart said.

"Sometimes the winner or somebody will take up a collection for him," Kilkenny added.

"If this Sandoval is to fight Turner, how come you figure to get a fight with him?"

Kilkenny shrugged. "I've a notion Sandoval won't show up at the last minute and they'll need somebody else." He smiled, looking over at Ma. "Friends can be very helpful."

"You got more guts than I'd have," O'Hara said. "Turner's a tiger in the ring. I've still got a copy of the *Police Gazette* somewhere around with a picture of him."

At that moment, oddly enough, Kilkenny remembered Cain Brockman.

On that desperate day back in the Live Oak country of Texas, he had killed Abel Brockman and Cain had been thrown from his horse and knocked unconscious. Later, in the Trail House, he had whipped Cain in a knock-down and drag-out fight. Cain had sworn to kill him, and now Cain Brockman was coming to Cedar . . . was probably there, in fact.

When night came, Kilkenny threw his saddle on a slim black gelding and rode out of the Cup. He was going to see Nita. Even as he rode, he admitted to himself there was little reason for seeing her except that it was what he wanted. He had no right to take chances with his life when it was so important to so many other people who were depending on him. He wanted to see Nita, but he also wanted some indication of what was happening in town.

He rode swiftly, and the black horse was eager for the trail. He wasn't Buck, but he was a good night horse, chosen for that quality when night-herding cattle. Some horses take to night work and others do not, and the black seemed born to it. Moreover, the horse was fast, with speed to spare.

It was very late when he rode up to the outskirts of Cedar, and his thoughts reverted to Leathers, whom he had awakened from a sound sleep, and to Dan Cooper, the tough cowhand-gunman who had been watching Leathers' store. Cooper was a good man on the wrong side, while Leathers was one who would try always to be on the winning side and who had no loyalty but to himself.

Leaving his horse in the shadow of an empty building near the Crystal Palace where he could stand under the trees and out of sight, Kilkenny studied the Palace for some time, listening to the night sounds and getting his ears accustomed to the normal sounds so he could quickly pick up anything out of the ordinary.

Ghostlike then, he moved along the back of the buildings to the door he sought. It was locked.

Ahead of him a curtain was stirred by the wind, a curtain indicating an open window. He paused near it, listening. Inside he could hear the breathing of a man, yet it was the only way in. Hesitating only a moment, he put his foot over the sill and ducked his head through the window.

He drew his other foot in and straightened up, only to be suddenly seized from behind. A powerful forearm came across his throat in a stranglehold, crushing back against his throat with tremendous power. He strained forward, agonizing pain shooting through the growing blackness and desperation in his brain, and then he leaned forward, lifting the man's feet clean from the floor. Suddenly the hold relaxed and he felt a hand slide down his side and touch his gun butt, then the other.

"I am sorry, señor," a voice whispered. "I did not know it was you."

"Brigo!"

"Sí. I did not know you, señor, but when you lifted me from the ground . . . only one man is as powerful as you, señor. Then, your guns, I know them well."

"The señorita is here?"

"Sí. Señor, it is good that you come. I fear for her. Thees Hale, he wants her ver' much! Also, the Cub of the Bear. He wants her. I fear for her. One day they will come for her. This I know. And I am but one man, señor."

There was worry in the big man's tone, and Kilkenny knew it was not for himself. Caring for Nita Riordan was for him a sacred trust.

"I see the two hombres Dunn and Ravitz. They watch me always. Soon they will try to keel me. I think the Cub of the Bear has instructed them to do so.

"The señorita, she has told me to do nothing unless they move first, but I cannot wait longer. Together they might kill me or hurt me so that I cannot watch over her, so I must go out and hunt them . . . with the blade, señor."

He paused. "You are a man of the wars, señor. You understand what must be done."

"Wait, if you can. Then do what you must. You do not kill without reason, Jaime. That I know. Do not wait for the

señorita to tell you, because she will not. Even what she knows
must be done will not be done because of her heart.

"We know that, Jaime. But there are men out there who
have no heart, who do not care. Cub is one. When the time
comes, do what you must."

"I am a Yaqui, señor. You weel come with me?"

On cat feet Kilkenny followed the big man down the hall,
where he tapped very lightly on a door. Immediately she said,
"Brigo?"

"*Sí*. The señor ees here."

The door opened quickly, and Jaime Brigo vanished in the
darkness down the hall as Kilkenny stepped into the room.

He heard her draw the curtains, heard the strike of a match,
and then a lighted candle. There were Tiffany lamps in the
room, but she did not light one; the candle was easier, quicker,
and more portable.

Her black hair fell over her shoulders halfway to her waist.
He saw the quick rise of her breast under the thin material of
the nightgown. "Kilkenny? What is it?"

Her voice was low, and something in the timbre made his
muscles tremble, and it was all he could do not to take her in
his arms.

"I had to see you. You are all right?"

"He has given me until after the celebration to make up my
mind. After that I must marry him or escape somehow." She
put the candle down. "Lance, I honestly do not think he has
any doubt. He can see no reason why a woman would not be
eager to marry him, especially such a one as I . . . who keeps a
saloon."

"That celebration is the cornerstone of everything now."
Briefly, dispassionately, he related what had taken place, the
crossing of the wilderness country, the fights at Blazer, and the
ambush on the road. The deaths of Miller, Soderman, and
Gaddis, as well as those of Lije and the others.

"He's made the greatest mistake of his life," he added,
"although he doesn't know it yet. Hale is in deep trouble now."

He removed his hat quickly. "Sorry, I wasn't thinking."
Then he asked, "Has he said anything about Blazer?"

"From all you say, I am sure he doesn't know all that
happened. He said there would be an attempt to get food from
there but that it couldn't be done. He seemed well pleased
with his plans."

"I'm going to fight Turner," Kilkenny said.

"I know."

"If Sandoval doesn't show up, that is."

"I talked to Mrs. Hatfield. You can be sure that he will not be here. I had heard he had a girl in San Francisco, so he got a ticket to there and a suggestion that there was going to be a lot of trouble, and some shooting, and that even if he won he might not get his money. He decided to go to San Francisco, but King Bill doesn't know it yet."

"What will he do?"

"He'll be furious. That fight is the big event of the celebration, and he particularly wishes to make a friend of Halloran. I do not know all his reasons, but I know Hale is disturbed about some new territorial ruling."

Kilkenny nodded. "Nita, I know nothing about that ruling or Halloran, but I do know that once I speak to him, Hale is finished. It is simple as that. But that is why I must speak to him, and there'll be no other way to even get close to him unless I am in that ring."

"All right," she said simply, "when Sandoval fails to show, I'll suggest you. I think he will do it."

She turned back to him. "Lance, are you sure you want to do this? I've seen Turner. He is here in town training right now. I have seen him bend silver dollars in his fingers, and the other evening he squatted beside one of the tables, with dishes and food on it, and he took the corner of the table in his teeth and lifted all four legs off the floor."

"He's strong. There's no question of it. And he's a very good fighter. But I have to speak to Halloran, and my only chance is from the ring. I must convince him that we are not outlaws, and I have one argument of which Hale knows nothing, but I must talk to Halloran."

"Brigo says you will win."

"Win?" For the first time he thought seriously of that, yet the big Yaqui had an almost animal instinct for judging the fighting abilities of men. A fierce, ruthless man himself, he had lived long in a land where men lived only by courage and strength.

"Nita, if there is a chance, say something to Halloran."

"There won't be. He will see to that. Hale trusts no one except Cub. Yet, if the chance comes, I shall say what I can."

He turned and put a hand on the knob. "Nita, when this is over, I am coming for you. I have waited too long."

"I will be ready." She looked up at him in the dim light.

"Wherever you go, I will go. I made my choice, Lance, long ago in Texas."

Kilkenny slipped from the house and returned to his horse. The black was eager to go. When he mounted he did not return the way he had come but right down the main street. He had to see the ring, see where the seats would be.

The ring was regulation twenty-four feet. At one side, where it would be shaded from the afternoon sun, was a booth containing several chairs. It was draped with bunting. Undoubtedly this was where Hale would sit with Cub and his guests. The emperor to watch the gladiators. Kilkenny smiled. "And to observe his destruction," he said aloud.

A light footstep, and Lance turned the black sharply, his right hand ready.

"It's all right, Kilkenny." A man stepped from the shadows near the ring. "It's Dan Cooper."

"You know me, then?"

Cooper chuckled. "Recognized your face that first day but couldn't place it. Matter of fact, it came to me just now. Hale will be wild when he hears."

"You're a good man, Cooper," Kilkenny said, "but on the wrong side."

"When is the winning side the wrong side? It isn't for me. I'm not making any statements as to who is right and who isn't, but for a gunhand, the best side is always the winning side."

"No conscience, Cooper?" Kilkenny asked mildly. "Dick Moffit was a good man, so were Tot Wilson, Lije Hatfield, and Jody Miller."

"Lije died?" Cooper asked quickly. "Damn the luck! I was hoping he'd make it. The Hales don't think much of the Hatfields, but they don't know that mountain stock like I do. Now they will have to kill every last one of them or die themselves."

"You could have tried a shot at me, Cooper."

"From the dark? I'm not that kind. I'm not anxious to be the man who shoots you, anyway. Somebody will do it someday, and then he will be 'the man who shot Kilkenny,' and every punk would-be hotshot in the country will be taking shots at him."

Dan Cooper walked closer. "Kilkenny, there's talk around town—just rumor, mind you—that Sandoval isn't going to show, and that you're going to fight Turner."

"Now, how did that story get started? Makes a man wonder, doesn't it?"

"It's a fact, Kilkenny. Also, nobody is repeating the rumor to King Bill." Cooper put his hand on the black's neck. "That's the trouble with being king, you're always the last one to hear what everybody else is saying."

"What are they saying?"

"I heard today there'd been a fight in the mountains, and a lot of killing done. Would you know anything about that, Kilkenny?"

"We sent a couple of wagons through to Blazer. An effort was made to stop them. They went through and came back."

"That was it, then. We heard Lije Hatfield was shot, but nothing more. Whoever was responsible isn't anxious to tell Hale."

"Soderman was responsible, and Soderman won't be telling him. Nor Gaddis, either."

"Gaddis was asking for it, but Soderman? I thought he'd be too smart to get himself killed."

"I gave Rye Pitkin his walking papers," Kilkenny said, "and I think he's gone."

"I'll be damned! And your wagons went through?"

"Cooper, take my advice and fork your bronc. Just take out of here and don't come back. Hale is through."

"*Hale?*" Cooper shook his head. "Why, Kilkenny, this won't stop him! Not even your name won't. He's got the money and he has the power—"

"Not anymore, he hasn't."

"What do you mean by that?"

"Dan, sometimes a man's ego gets so inflated that he just can't see other people. Anybody who has less than he has is nobody, and to be brushed aside.

"Well, Hale brushed a man aside the other day who will haunt him the rest of his life. I am going to help grease the skids for Hale, Dan, but he destroyed himself when one of his gunmen shot Jody Miller."

"Jody Miller? That farmer?" Cooper was puzzled. "I don't get it."

Kilkenny turned the black. "Like I said, Dan. Get up in the saddle and ride—far and fast."

"No, I'll stay. Anyway, I want to see the fight. If you do tackle Turner, I wouldn't miss it for the world. Between the two of us, I wouldn't envy you. That hombre isn't human. He eats like three men, and muscles? He's got muscles on his muscles!"

Kilkenny started away.

"Just two people in town bettin' on you, Kilkenny."

Lance drew up. "Who?"

"That Yaqui gunfighter and Cain Brockman."

"Brockman?" Kilkenny was surprised.

"He says he's goin' to kill you, but not until you've whipped Turner. Fact is, he told Turner to his face that if you two met you would whip him."

Dan Cooper hitched up his belt. "You'd better ride on, Kilkenny. My relief will be comin' along soon, and he might not be so anxious to see a good fight that he would pass up five thousand dollars."

"Five thousand?"

"That's what it's worth to anybody who brings you in, dead or alive. That's off the record, of course. Cub didn't like it. He wants you himself."

"So long, Dan."

"*Adios,* but watch out for Cub. He's faster'n a striking rattler."

Kilkenny rode out of town and took to the hills. He did not follow a trail, but as the moon was up, he chose mountain-sides and streambeds. He bedded down about daylight in a hidden hollow in the hills he had found while hunting. He slept until almost noon.

When he awakened he got up and climbed into the saddle again. So Cain Brockman had bet on him. As he rode he lived over again that bitter, bloody afternoon in the old Trail House when he had whipped Cain. Cain's great body had seemed impervious to anything a fist could do, yet Lance had finally brought him down.

He had taken a roundabout route, so it was almost sundown before he rode into the Cup. Parson and Quince were waiting for him.

He told them the results of his ride and of his talk with Dan Cooper.

"You're dead set on fightin' Turner?"

"It's our only chance to get to Halloran. If I can talk to him, we've got it made. Halloran will open a full-scale investigation of just what's been going on."

"You think he'll listen? Halloran, I mean?"

"He will. He will listen and he will give me all his attention, believe me."

"What if Turner beats you insensible before you get a chance to talk?"

"That's a chance I have to take, but I've changed my mind about a couple of things. I was going in just to fight him until I got a chance to talk. Now I'm going in to win."

Parson shook his head, then spat. "Ain't the fight has me worried. If the good Lord wants you to win, you'll win. I'm worried about what comes after.

"Win or lose, do you think Hale will let you ride out of town scot-free?"

SIXTEEN

In a small alcove off the gaming room, at a beautifully set table, Nita Riordan was entertaining King Bill Hale, Cub, Wallace, and Halloran when John Bartlett appeared.

"Mr. Hale? May I speak with you, sir?"

"John? By all means, come in. Have a seat. Gentlemen, John Bartlett is the business manager for our fighter, Tombull Turner."

He turned to Nita. "Nita, I am sorry. Mr. Bartlett, Nita Riordan."

"We have met," Bartlett said. "I've had the pleasure."

He was a big red-haired man of florid face and quiet manners, but now he was disturbed. "Mr. Hale, I've just had word that Sandoval won't be here. He's gone off to San Francisco!"

"*What?*" Hale was furious. "Why, that . . ." He stopped abruptly.

"You mean there's to be no fight?" Halloran protested. "I'd been looking forward to it."

"I've tried, but there doesn't seem to be another fighter within miles. There's some miner in Butte, but nobody knows much about him and it would take several days to get him here."

Hale leaned over the table. "John, think of somebody! We can set up fresh horses and rush him in here."

"John C. Heenan is in New York. Tom Sayers is supposed to be on his way back to England. There is nobody around who could even hope to give Tombull a match."

"There might be," Nita said quietly.

Hale either did not hear or chose to ignore her. "The miner you spoke of. Can he fight?"

"As a matter of fact . . . no. He's big, strong, and that's about it. I doubt if he could stand up for a round."

Halloran turned to Nita. "You know of someone?"

"Well, Mr. Hale knows him, and so does about everybody

124

else around here. He's not a professional, but he is a fighter, and a very good one."

"What about it, Hale?" Wallace said. "After all, you promised us a fight."

Hale hesitated, but Cub broke in. "Turner would beat him to death, and I'd like to see it."

"The man's not a professional," Hale protested.

"But he's good, is that it?" Wallace insisted.

"There's already talk around town," Nita interposed quietly. "That newcomer, Cain Brockman? You saw him. He believes Trent could beat Turner."

"Who is this Brockman? Is he around?" Bartlett asked.

"The big man standing at the bar . . . the man with the broken nose and the red vest. That's Brockman."

"Can we talk to him, Mr. Hale? After all, I've brought Turner up here at considerable expense. If there's a chance of a fight, we should have it."

"The man's an outlaw!" Hale said irritably. "He's one of that bunch up in the hills that I've been telling you about. I know nothing about him."

Bartlett got up from the table and walked over to Cain Brockman. After a minute he came back, followed by Brockman.

"Do you know this man they call Trent?" Bartlett asked him.

"I know him."

"We need to know only one thing about him," Halloran suggested. "Can he fight?"

"If you mean can he whip Turner, I've got five hundred dollars says he can." Cain leaned his big fists on the table. "I came here to kill him, and I intend to, but he can fight.

"Nobody ever whupped me until he did it. I had many a fight on tie-cutting camps, railroad-construction camps, everywhere. I whupped ever'body. That man you call Trent weighs less'n two hundred. I weigh two-sixty. I got four inches in height on him, and the reach, and he whupped me."

"What more do you want?" Nita said quietly. "You need a fighter, and you have one. What difference does it make, Mr. Hale, whether he's run out of here before the fight or after it?"

Hale still hesitated, and Wallace looked around curiously at Cain. "You said you came here to kill him. Why?"

"He killed my brother, Abel. Shot him dead."

"Was it a gun battle?" Halloran asked.

"It was fair shootin', if that's what you're askin', an' it'll be a fair shootin' when I kill him."

"What about it, Hale?" Halloran said. "Is this man our fighter?"

John Bartlett was waiting. King Bill Hale did not like it. He wanted to see Trent whipped, and whipped badly, but he did not want the man in town, he did not want him acknowledged or recognized or given attention. He wanted him dead. At the same time, he had invited these men here to see a fight. He had imported John Bartlett and his fighter for the purpose.

"I don't know how we can get him," he said after a moment. "That's a lawless crowd up there."

"I could send my man Brigo after him. He's a neutral party."

King Bill was irritated. Why didn't she stay out of this? She and Cub.

"All right," he said, "if we can get him."

"I'm genuinely curious about the man now," Wallace said. "He must be quite a fighter."

"Turner will kill him," Hale said irritably.

Cain Brockman reached in his pocket. "What odds are you givin'?"

Hale threw Brockman an angry look, but Cain was not awed. "I ain't one of your outfit, Mr. Hale, and I'm driftin' on after this here's over. I got five hundred on Trent at the odds."

Wallace glanced at Nita. "You run a gambling house. What odds would you give?"

"We will not be taking bets on the fight," she replied, "although we would be willing to hold stakes. Turner is a skilled professional who has fought many of the best. Trent is at best an amateur. He will be outweighed by at least thirty pounds. The odds should be ten to one, but I would say four to one."

"That seems fair," Halloran commented.

"I got five hundred at that price," Brockman said. "Five hundred in gold."

"I'll take it!" Cub said.

Nita Riordon looked up at Brockman. "Will you ask Price to step over here? He'll record the bet and we will hold stakes."

Hale turned his back to the room and filled his glass. He was profoundly irritated. The last thing he wanted was that man Trent coming into town now, fight or no fight, yet he did not wish to throw his weight around in the presence of Halloran and Wallace. He needed them too much. If he could get the territory to ratify, in one way or another, his claim to the land he was holding, many of his problems would be settled. Before any further discussion came up, he would be in complete possession and he could get some of his hands to file on claims that he could then buy from them.

This was wild land, grazing land, and there were millions of acres unclaimed, largely unwanted. It was coming into the possession of various men by a variety of means, and many of their claims would not stand in court, but for the time being they had possession. With the cattle business what it was, and beef prices in the mining camps what they were, a man could double and even triple his money in three or four years.

Halloran sat back in his chair and bit the end from a cigar. "Well, that's a relief! We will at least have our fight, Hale, and we're lucky to have this man so close by." He glanced at Hale again. "I take it you don't like him?"

"I do not," Hale said flatly.

The crowds started coming into Cedar before daylight. There were miners from Silver City, a contingent from Mountain City, and even one from Florence. They camped outside of town, filled the hotels, crowded the bars. The gold camps had been abandoned for the day, for entertainment of any kind was scarce, and an excuse to come to town and let off some steam was sorely needed.

There was much talk around town. Turner was a known man, Trent was not. The odds mounted and Jaime Brigo got his money down at six to one.

So far as Lance knew, only three people in town knew him as Kilkenny. Perhaps four. And that was the way he wanted it.

He knew what he had to do, and he knew that once he spoke to Halloran, the man would listen. He had that to tell him which would grip his attention.

Kilkenny rode into town when the sun was high. For over an hour he had been lying out in the hills watching the movements through his glasses. He was sure that King Bill would avoid trouble today. There were too many visitors, too many people who lived beyond his control. He would be wanting to make the best impression as what he believed himself to be—an honest, upright citizen.

Brigo had ridden into the Cup with Nita's message and the story of Cain Brockman's bet. Kilkenny was to report to John Bartlett in the Crystal Palace.

Kilkenny rode into town with Parson Hatfield and Quince. Steve Runyon and O'Hara had come in more than an hour

before, and O'Hara had immediately fallen in with several old
friends from the mines in Silver City, several Irish miners with
whom he had worked laying track for the Central Pacific. Only
a few of the Hale riders knew any of the hill men by sight.

Pushing through the batwing doors, Kilkenny took in the big
room at a glance, a skill developed from long practice and an
awareness that enemies might be anywhere. The place was
crowded and all the games going full blast.

Nita Riordan was known as a decent woman, but she was
also beautiful, and in a hard land with too little of feminine
grace or beauty, many men came just to look. She had an easy,
friendly way, permitted no liberties, but had a word for everyone. She had developed an excellent memory and knew very
well how people liked to be remembered, so here and there
she would stop to ask a man how his claim was doing, how
deep he had gone, or how the drought was affecting the range.
Here and there she had a word about a favored horse, and
those men whose families she knew of were always asked about
them.

In all of this, both Price Dixon and Jaime Brigo had been of
help, for both were good listeners and reported to her what
they had heard. The bartenders passed through her office each
evening, relating what they had heard.

She was in no sense wishing to pry, but she had learned
from her father, and from observation since, that the West was
a lonely place. Many men had no one, others had left families
back east until they could establish themselves; men more
often than not rode alone, worked alone, and lived alone, doing
their own cooking. A friendly word and a few minutes of
conversation with someone who seemed interested outdid all
the glitter and the spangles that some other places tried to
provide.

Kilkenny glimpsed Brigo across the room, tilted back in his
usual chair. Their eyes met in brief acknowledgment, and then
Kilkenny saw Price Dixon. He was dealing cards at a nearby
table.

There was a scarcely perceptible warning in Dixon's eyes
and a slight movement of the head toward the bar. Kilkenny
felt a chill.

Cain Brockman was at the bar, a huge man in plaid pants,
boots with Mexican spurs, a black coat, red vest, and a black
flat-brimmed hat like the one he himself wore. Cain was watching him.

Almost instinctively men sensed the sudden tension. In a land and a time when gunfights exploded without warning, men had learned to sense impending trouble and get out of the way. Eyes began to lift, seeing the tall, broad-shouldered man who had entered and the huge figure of the man in the red vest at the bar.

Kilkenny walked between the tables to the bar. A deadly hush gripped the room. Already Brockman's statement that he had come to town to kill the man called Trent was well known, and this newcomer must be the man.

Cain's broad, strong-boned face still carried the scars of their fight, and Kilkenny was well aware that the man was dangerous as a wounded grizzly. That he had whipped him once meant nothing, for Cain was a fighter and would fight again. Moreover, the big man was one of the best men with a gun Kilkenny had ever seen.

Through narrowed eyes Brockman watched Kilkenny come across the room toward him, noting the ease and the grace of the man. Unseen, Nita Riordan had come into the room, watching Kilkenny as he approached Brockman.

"Been a long time, Cain," Kilkenny said.

"Too long."

"I hear you've come to town to kill me, Cain." He spoke quietly, but in the deadly hush the words were heard distinctly in all parts of the room. "If we shoot it out, I'm going to kill you, Cain, but you're a good man with a gun and you'll surely get some lead into me.

"I've come to ask you to hold off. As you may have heard, I'm supposed to fight Tombull Turner. That's going to be trouble enough without carrying a craw full of lead when I do it. So how about a truce until the fight's over?"

Cain hesitated. His small gray eyes were chill and cold, but there came into them a light of reluctant admiration. A mild humor came over his face and he said, "I can wait. Let it never be said that Cain Brockman broke up a good fight. Besides," he added, "I've got money on you. Nobody knows more about your fightin' ability than me."

"It's a deal, then? Until after the fight?" Kilkenny held out his hand.

"It's a deal," Cain agreed and they shook.

Somebody cheered, and then they all did. Flushed and a little embarrassed by the sudden attention, Brockman turned his back on the crowd and tossed off his drink.

Kilkenny turned and walked back to Price Dixon, who was now standing near his table with a big red-headed man.

He was nearing them when the doors pushed open and King Bill Hale entered, with Cub right behind him, and behind them the Gold Dust Twins, Dunn and Ravitz.

Ignoring them, Kilkenny walked up to Bartlett. "I'm Trent," he said.

"Pleasure." Bartlett's cool eyes took in the wide shoulders and the easy movements and approved. "You know me?"

"I've seen you several times. In New Orleans and in Abilene."

"Then you've seen Turner fight?" Bartlett asked quickly.

"Yes, I've seen him. He's good."

"And you're not worried? He nearly killed Tom Hanlon."

Kilkenny smiled. "And who was Hanlon? A big chunk of beef so slow he couldn't get out of his tracks."

"Then you will actually fight Turner?" Bartlett was surprised, but pleased.

"Fight him? I'm going to whip him!"

"That's the way to talk!" A black-bearded miner shoved himself close. "I'm sick of this Tombull Turner struttin' around like he was cock of the walk. My money goes on Trent or whatever your name is."

"Mine, too!" another miner said. "I'd rather you was a miner, but my money's on you even if you are nursin' cows!"

Kilkenny smiled at him. "Friend, I've swung a single or double jack in almost as many mines as you have, and dipped a pan in half the creeks in the country."

Bartlett interposed. "Look, this fight is for a thousand dollars, winner-take-all, the money put up by Mr. Hale, here. But if you'd like to make a side bet . . ."

Kilkenny reached into his shirt pocket and took out a fat wad of bills. "I do want to bet," he said, "and I understand that Mr. Hale is giving odds of four to one. I have five thousand dollars here."

"That's more than I can cover," Bartlett said.

"It was my impression"—Kilkenny was purposely speaking a little louder—"that Hale was offering four-to-one odds and covering all bets."

Hale was angered and embarrassed. He was not a gambling man and had no intention of betting on the fight, but he had been trapped into one bet and now he was being led into another; to back out now would look like welshing, and the story would go all over the country.

Moreover, if he did bet and Kilkenny won, then Hale would scarcely dare order him killed, because all would believe it was revenge for his losses. Hale was no fool and was quick to see he had been trapped; nor at the moment could he see any clear way out of it except, of course, that Turner would win.

The thought brought relief. Of course Turner would win! And *he* would win, and this man called Trent would lose, and if he made more trouble, it would seem that he was doing so purely out of malice.

"I'm calling you, Hale. Five thousand dollars at your own odds, four to one. Put up or shut up."

Hale still hesitated, and all in the room were listening. Coldly furious, he started to speak, but Kilkenny spoke first.

"Backing down, Hale? Or don't you believe Turner can whip me? Have you decided the man who whipped you on your own ground can whip Turner, too?"

"No!" Hale spoke angrily. "I'm covering your bet, and no fence-crawling nester can talk to me that way! Win or lose, when the fight is over, you get out! *Out!* Do you hear me?"

A miner booed, and then the room did. Cub turned on them, his face white and angry. Seeing his face, Kilkenny had the sudden feeling that Cub Hale was insane. It was only a fleeting impression, but it left him cold and wary. He must be careful. Cub's reactions might not be those of a normal man.

Partly it was that King Bill had been top dog ever since Cub could remember. He had carried himself like a king, had owned or possessed vast acreage, and everyone spoke to him with respect. Cub had grown up with a sense of his father's unlimited power. His father's, and hence his own, as his father's surrogate.

Now that power had been challenged by men whom Cub saw as nothing more than the dirt beneath his feet.

When they were outside in the street, Parson Hatfield commented, "You made King Bill look mighty bad in there. You made some friends, too."

"*We* made friends. That's what's important. We've got to make more friends, Parson. Don't ever forget that the opinion of those people out there is what matters. People will tolerate such a man as Hale only so long, and if we get enough friends, we have a fighting chance.

"Hale can win only so long as he can make what he's doing seem right. He's painted our picture as rustlers and interlopers, people crowding on his land, although he never had claimed it and never explains how it came to be his.

"If it stopped right here and Hale had me killed or took my land, there would be a lot of questions asked, and Hale would have to come up with answers. We've got to make friends in the areas around Cedar, places Hale can't touch. They'll remember what I said today.

"We've got something going for us. We're a few poor people bucking a powerful and a wealthy man. In this fight I am the underdog. I'm a cowhand and miner fighting a trained prizefighter with my fists, and a good part of that crowd is going to be with me. Some of them will be Hale's own people.

"Whenever a man becomes so arrogant, even many of those who work for him and take his money will dislike him. They dare say nothing, but I'd bet a little money that some of his own people will be wanting me to win."

O'Hara came up beside him. "We found a room where you can lie down an' rest up a bit," he said, "and you'd best do it. That fight may last for hours.

"Back in 1856 in Australia James Kelly and Jack Smith fought for six hours and fifteen minutes."*

The room wasn't much, but the bed was a good one. O'Hara drew the blinds and left the room, and Kilkenny pulled off his boots, hung his gun belts over the back of a chair, and stretched out. He knew he could not sleep, but he did.

---

*In 1893 Andy Bowen and Jack Burke fought 110 rounds, in seven hours and nineteen minutes in New Orleans. It was called a draw when neither man could continue. But this was after the conversation above.

SEVENTEEN

It was midafternoon when Lance Kilkenny walked down to the ring. The balconies of the Crystal Palace and the Mecca were crowded, as were the rooftops and the top of the corral fence. The intervening space had been filled with chairs right to the ringside. The miners from Silver City were there in full strength, and others had come down by stage from Florence and some neighboring mining towns.

The bunting-decorated booth near the ring was empty and two men guarded it to keep interlopers out.

Kilkenny climbed into the ring and stripped to the waist. He had no trunks or tights so was wearing a pair of buckskin breeches and moccasins that fitted snugly. On hand he had a pair of skintight gloves ready to put on as soon as they could be examined by the opposing seconds to ascertain that they were not weighted or doctored in any way.

O'Hara draped an Indian blanket over Kilkenny's shoulders, and he sat down on the stool.

A roar from the gathered crowd told him that Tombull Turner was coming. Turner climbed through the ropes, never wasting a glance on Kilkenny. This was his business, and he was about to go about it. Who or what his opponent was made no difference. His job was to go out and get him with the least trouble possible.

"Lance?" It was Price Dixon. "I've had some experience as a handler, if you will trust a gambling man."

"We're all gamblers, more or less. I'd appreciate it, Price. O'Hara here knows a little, but he will be the first to tell you he's had no experience."

Kilkenny stood up to stretch his legs and look carefully around. Parson Hatfield and Runyon sat right behind his corner. Jesse and Saul Hatfield were, rifles in hand, one on the

133

roof of the Palace, one the Mecca. Quince Hatfield sat behind Turner's corner.

Suddenly the crowd parted and King Bill Hale came striding to his box, closely followed by Cub Hale with Wallace and Halloran. Behind them were Dunn and Ravitz.

Almost at the same time Nita Riordan came from the Palace accompanied by Jaime Brigo, and they joined Hale in his booth, Brigo taking up a position behind it near the Gold Dust Twins.

John Bartlett walked across the ring to Kilkenny. "Look," he said, "we haven't been able to find a referee, and they've asked me. Now, I am associated with Turner, but I—"

"You've the reputation of being an honest man," Kilkenny said, "an honest man in a game where there have been too few. So why not?"

"Good! Come to the center of the ring, then."

Turner was thirty pounds heavier, taller, longer of arm. His arms and shoulders were heavy with muscle, almost too heavy for the kind of speed he would need, Kilkenny thought.

"London prize-ring rules," Bartlett said. "When a man goes down, that's the end of the round, whether he's knocked down, thrown down, or falls down. No hitting below the belt, no eye-gouging."

Tombull *was* big, and he was obviously in the best shape a man could be. His deltoid development was massive, his stomach was flat, his legs were columns of muscle.

Kilkenny was lean and dark. He had the strength of years of hard work with ax or rope, wrestling steers, riding wild broncs, felling timber, and using a crosscut saw. Actually he weighed two hundred pounds but was built so compactly that people regularly estimated his weight at twenty pounds less.

"All right," Bartlett said, "go to your corners, then come to scratch and go to fighting. Any man who fails to toe the scratch at the beginning of a round loses."

They turned away, and then Kilkenny stopped. "One thing, Bartlett, on your qualifications as a referee."

Bartlett stopped, surprised. Turner stopped, too, turning half-around and frowning.

"What's that?" Bartlett said sharply.

Kilkenny's expression was innocent. "Can you count up to ten, sir? In a loud enough tone so that Turner will hear it, even though half-conscious? I want him to have every chance."

Bartlett smiled, glancing at Turner. "Don't worry about me. I always count loud!"

Turner was furious. He had turned toward his corner, but Kilkenny toed the scratch. "Come on, Turner, let's not keep them waiting!"

Turner wheeled and started back, and the timekeeper hurriedly shouted "Time!" as Turner threw his first punch. He was angry at this never-heard-of upstart and threw the punch too soon, and Kilkenny beat him to the punch with a jab to the mouth.

The speed and force of the punch startled the bigger man, and he stopped dead in his tracks just in time to catch a looping right to the ear. Turner crowded and grabbed Kilkenny with the intent of throwing him to the floor, but Kilkenny hooked hard to the head and Turner let him go, smashing away with both hands. For a moment the two men stood toe to toe and swapped punches, but Kilkenny broke off. Against a larger, stronger man, that was nonsense. If he won, or even stayed in, he must do so through skill, and nothing else.

Turner let go with a left that caught Kilkenny in the chest, knocking him into the ropes. Turner came after him, and Kilkenny got in close and landed twice to the body. If he won this fight, it would be just that way, and he knew it.

Turner came in, feinted a left, and caught Kilkenny with a right. Groggy and hurt, Kilkenny fell into the ropes, and Turner was on him at once, punching with both hands. Clinching, Lance hung on tight, then saw his chance and back-heeled Turner, flipping him to the floor, ending the round.

"He hits hard," he said grimly.

"Box him," Price said. "Don't try to mix it up with him." He sponged off Kilkenny's face. "Take your time out there, now. There's no hurry."

He was still dazed when they came to scratch for the second round, but as Turner came in, Lance struck quickly with a left that landed on the side of the neck. Turner took it coming in, clubbed Kilkenny with a right and left, pushed him off, and threw a hard right that Kilkenny slipped inside of, landing a right to the body.

Turner clubbed the right to the head again, and Kilkenny dug a left into the midsection and then a right to the heart. Turner caught him, spun him and hit him, then grabbed him suddenly and slammed him to the canvas to end the second round.

Both men came to scratch quickly for the third round, and
Turner landed a left and a right that shook Kilkenny to his
heels. The bigger man could really hit, and he was showing it.
In a clinch, out of the corners of his eyes, Kilkenny located the
two men with Hale. They were seated side by side with Hale
in the front row, not more than six feet from the ropes.

Turner was rough and strong. He tried to twist Kilkenny's
arm in a clinch, and Kilkenny got a forearm under his chin and
thrust his head up and back, then hit him with a glancing left.
Turner bulled him to the ropes, punching with both hands.

Tombull moved in, landing a left to the head, then a right to
the body. Kilkenny circled away, stabbing with his left. Turner
crowded him to the ropes, and when Kilkenny tried to sidestep
out of the corner, nailed him with a right that stopped Kilkenny
half-turned. Instantly Turner was on him, punching hard with
both hands. One fist caught Kilkenny over the eye, another
crashed into the pit of his stomach. He landed two feeble
punches to Turner's body, but the bigger man clubbed him on
the kidneys with his right fist.

Kilkenny slipped away, and, fists poised, Turner crowded in.

He threw a punch to the head, and Kilkenny ducked the
right but caught a chopping blow with the left that started
blood flowing from a cut over the eye. Turner closed in, and
feinting, caught Kilkenny with a right and floored him.

Dixon worked over the eye rapidly and skillfully. Dazed
though he was, Kilkenny was amazed at Dixon's skill. "Watch
the right!" Dixon said. "It's poison! Move away to his left."

Kilkenny stepped up to scratch, then sidestepped to avoid a
rush and stabbed a left to the head. Turner closed in and
Kilkenny went under a right and smashed both fists to the
body. Then he was thrown and hit the canvas again.

He took his rest gratefully and came hesitantly to the scratch,
but as Turner came up he lunged suddenly and smashed both
hands to the chin. Staggered, Turner braced himself, but before he could recover, Kilkenny hit him a hard left to the
mouth, then drove a hard right to the body. Turner shook off
the punches and bored in, hitting with short, wicked punches.
Kilkenny sidestepped, stabbed another left to the head, and
sidestepped again. Angered at missing two blows, Turner stopped
flatfooted and started to speak, and Kilkenny swung a right
to the ribs.

Turner bored in, crowding Kilkenny and hitting with short,
wicked punches to the head and body. Kilkenny tasted blood

from a cut inside his mouth, smashed a right to the ribs in close, and then was literally hurled into the ropes. Turner came after him, and Kilkenny dropped his left hand to the top rope, and grasping it, ducked three hard punches in a row, then whipped an underhanded right to the ribs that stopped Turner in his tracks.

The crowd was on its feet, most of them yelling for Kilkenny. He moved away rapidly, making Turner follow, then stopped, feinted a left, and whipped another underhand right to the belly. Turner took it coming in, and Kilkenny saw he had hurt him, but before he could sidestep, Tombull caught him with an overhand right to the chin that dropped him to his knees, ending the round.

Tombull turned for his corner, and Lance got to his feet. He was almost in front of Hale's booth, and before anyone knew what he was doing, he stepped to the ropes. Blood was trickling from the cut over his eye.

"Gentlemen"—he spoke to Halloran and Wallace—"I am not a prizefighter. I am fighting because it is the only way I could get close enough to you to present my case. I am one of a dozen nesters who have filed on claims in the high peaks, claims from which King Bill Hale is unlawfully trying to drive us. Several of our men have been killed, brutally murdered because they refused to leave the land on which they filed—"

"Time!"

Kilkenny turned sharply and stepped to the scratch. Turner caught him with a hard right before he got straightened around, and he fell into the ropes. Unwilling to see him go down so quickly, Tombull rushed in and deliberately held Kilkenny up while smashing away at his body and head. Abruptly then, Turner stepped away and unleashed a powerful right.

Kilkenny almost fell, and he saw Turner getting set to let go with the right again, and Kilkenny knew he could not at that moment take another such punch. Nor had he finished his plea to Halloran.

He tried to duck, caught the second right as a glancing blow. Blasting pain hit him, and he saw the right coming again. With all his strength he tried to jerk free, but Turner intended to kill him now, and his jerk served only to make that blow miss.

In a daze, battered and beaten by a hurricane of blows, he glimpsed Cub Hale on his feet, hand on his gun. He saw Parson Hatfield facing him, and then Lance broke loose. Turner was on him like a madman, clubbing, striking with all his great strength, trying to batter Kilkenny so he could not rise again. The crowd was in an uproar, and he glimpsed Runyon behind Cub Hale with a gun on him, then he broke loose and crashed to the canvas.

O'Hara carried him bodily to his corner, where Dixon could work on him. A hefty inhalation of smelling salts and a few touches on his eye were all there was time for. They pushed him to his feet, and he made it to scratch, and then Tombull was on him, swinging punches with both hands, eager to finish the fight once and for all.

His very eagerness caused blows to miss that should have landed, and Kilkenny, weaving and swaying, retreating, using the ropes, clinching when he could do nothing else, weathered the storm.

Turner was fast for such a big man, and Kilkenny knew he had to slow him down. He feinted, Turner threw a punch, and he countered with the underhand right to the belly again. And then he hit him with it twice more, and spreading his legs, he began to swing with both hands. Toe to toe they stood, slugging it out, but Kilkenny, battered though he was, was still the faster with his punches. Suddenly he was lost to everything but the fury of the battle itself.

Tombull missed a hard-thrown right, and Kilkenny smashed a right to the ribs; then, sliding a right arm around the bigger man's bull neck, he proceeded to hold him in chancery while he battered his face with blow after blow.

Turner did a back somersault to break free and end the round.

Gasping for breath, every gasp like a stab in the ribs, Kilkenny stepped again to the ropes. "We were refused food for our families in Cedar! A wagon we sent to Blazer was waylaid and three of our men killed! One of those men was *Jody Miller!*"

"What?" Halloran was on his feet.

The call of time interrupted, and then Tombull Turner was on him, his face bloody and wild. Kilkenny, as though getting his message across had given him a second wind, faded away swiftly, avoiding Turner's attack.

He moved swiftly, easier now, and occasionally stabbed a left to the face, but refused to close. He had to whip the big man; men had bet on him, even Cain Brockman. He had gotten his message across, and now nothing Hale could do short of killing both officials could stop what was sure to happen. Yet now he had to win the fight, and to that he devoted all his attention.

Faster than the bigger man, he carried less weight and was less affected by the heat, which was well over ninety degrees. He put a left to the face and another whipping right to the ribs. Another left and another right. Turner caught him with a glancing left, and Kilkenny hit him in the body with a left.

Turner threw a hard right, but Kilkenny stepped inside with an uppercut that drove Tombull's head back. A left hook knocked him to the floor. It was the first clean knockdown he had scored, and he went to his corner quickly. A glance at the visitors' box showed all the men seated, but Runyon and Parson were there with guns, and he could see that Cub was burning with anger.

Turner was slow coming to scratch, and it was obvious that he was realizing for the first time that he could lose.

He led with a left, and Kilkenny drew away from it, feinting with his own left. Turner moved in fast, and Kilkenny met him with a stiff right to the body; then, in close, he hit him twice more to the body with jarring blows.

Turner landed a hard left, feinted, and threw a right that Kilkenny ducked. He liked that high, hard right, Turner did, and Kilkenny moved in, purposely carrying his left low. The right came, and Kilkenny went under it with a right to the body. A few minutes later it worked again; Turner hurt him with a left, crossed a jarring right to the head, but Kilkenny was growing in confidence. The man could hit, but so could Kilkenny, and there were no boxers around now like Jem Mace had been.

The crowd had been yelling like madmen, but now they were quiet, with only an occasional shout. Turner bored in, and Kilkenny hit him hard with the underhand right to the body. This time it stopped Turner dead still and his jaw dropped a little. The blow had hurt.

Kilkenny circled to Turner's left, avoiding his right. He was hit twice with the left, but some of the steam was gone from Tombull's blows because the constant battering around the body was beginning to sap his strength.

Kilkenny suddenly moved in, punching hard with both hands, and for a minute they slugged toe to toe, but then Turner began to back off. Abruptly Kilkenny eased the pressure and feinted with the left, dropping it low. The right came high and hard, and he threw an inside right cross that was beautifully timed. It caught Tombull Turner coming and right on the point of the chin. The big man's knees buckled, and Kilkenny hit him twice more before he could fall. Turner hit the canvas, made one spasmodic effort to rise, then lay still.

Bartlett hesitated, then started to count. Kilkenny backed into his own corner, and O'Hara raised up behind him. "I've got your guns," he whispered.

"Put them around me with the blanket," he replied, and caught the gun belts as O'Hara put them around him, only half-covered by the blanket.

He got the gloves off. His hands were swollen, but not badly, for the tight leather gloves had protected his fists. He worked his fingers. One thing he knew, he was in no shape to make any fast draws.

Glancing around, he saw Brigo hurrying Nita toward the Palace.

Saul, Jesse, and Quince had closed in around Parson, and Runyon was with O'Hara.

Bartlett raised his hand, proclaiming Kilkenny the winner, and the crowd cheered and cheered again. But already they were breaking up, sensing trouble.

"You fought a good fight, Trent," Bartlett said, "a mighty good fight. I never saw a better."

"I hope I never have to fight another," he replied sincerely.

The Hale cowhands suddenly began to gather, and the miners surged around Kilkenny. "Go where y' like, boy," one said, "we're with you all the way!"

Kilkenny turned and walked right at the crowding Hale riders, and sullenly they broke away, leaving a path through them. He walked up to King Bill Hale.

"I'll take twenty thousand dollars now," he said.

The big rancher was pale and his eyes as cold as ice. "The Crystal Palace," he muttered, half turning away. "That woman . . . she was holding stakes. The money's there." With a flash of anger he looked at Kilkenny. "Every damn cent of it, for all the good it will do you."

Halloran and Wallace stood slightly apart from Hale now. Lance turned to them. "Gentlemen, what I said in the ring is true. I wish you would examine our claims and Hale's."

"Was that true about Jody Miller? Is he dead?"

"I am sorry, Mr. Halloran, and even more sorry to have to tell you that way, but I was afraid you'd not believe what else I said. Yes, Jody Miller is dead. He was killed trying to bring food from Blazer to his family, killed by some of Hale's men. I might add that several of those men have already paid the price."

Halloran turned on Hale. "You had Miller killed?"

"I had nobody killed! If he was killed, he was asking for it, settling on my land. He was nothing but trash! Trash, I say!"

"Jody Miller," Halloran said quietly, "was married to my sister. He was as likely a young man as I know. And as honest.

"I can promise you, Hale, there will be an investigation in the territorial courts, and you had better be prepared to answer questions, a lot of questions."

Kilkenny was watching Cub. The younger Hale's face was white; he stared from one to the other, unbelieving. The total power of his father in which he had come to believe was crumbling before his eyes. His father was standing there saying nothing. His father was taking it. Why didn't he smash them? Smash them all?

Kilkenny turned abruptly. "Let's go!" he said softly. He glanced around at the miners who stood ready to back him. "It's all right, boys, and thanks!"

"You needn't thank us!" one said. "We all had bets ridin' on you. We made a pile!"

Quickly they went to the house on the edge of town where they had rested briefly, and picked up their things. "I'll get the money, boys, and then we'll ride. Be prepared to ride fast!"

"What can they do now?" Runyon demanded. "We got our story across."

"And when it comes to trial, suppose all the witnesses are dead?" Kilkenny suggested. "We are in worse trouble now than ever. For a while, at least."

Nita was waiting for him. She had his money in a canvas bag.

"Cain Brockman was around to collect his. I asked if he still intended to kill you, but he wouldn't talk about it."

"We're getting out fast." Kilkenny explained his fears. "If you need help, just send a man into the mountains."

"I'd better ride with you," Dixon said. "My life wouldn't be worth a plugged nickel around here now."

"Get your horse," Kilkenny said. Then he turned. "Nita? If you want to, you can come."

"Not yet. I've a few things that need doing. Jaime is here. He will take care of me, and my men at the Palace. They are all loyal."

"Be careful. Very careful." He paused. "If you need help, run up one of those checkered tablecloths on the flagstaff and I'll come a-running."

They rode hard and fast, taking to little-known game trails

through the mountains. Kilkenny rode with his rifle in his
hands, ready for immediate use. They took to a dim trail along
the bottom of a steep-walled canyon, went up a switchback trail
toward the peaks, keeping under cover whenever possible.

Kilkenny was under no misapprehensions about King Bill.
Hale had been defeated a second time, he had lost a good bit of
money, and he had lost his bid for friends at the territorial
capital. Yet he was far from defeated, still a very wealthy man
with his retainers all about him, and somehow he would have
to prove to both Cedar and himself that he was still the king.
The one thing that could do it without question was the utter
annihilation of the squatters in the peaks. If Hale did not come
to that conclusion himself, Cub was there to suggest it.

Hale would have lost much. Knowing the man and knowing
the white lightning that lay beneath the surface of Cub Hale,
he guessed that the older man had more than once cautioned
the slower, surer way when Cub's total desire would have been
a shoot-out. Since childhood Cub had scarcely been restrained,
taking what he wanted and growing more arrogant by the year.

Whenever they came, Cub would be leading them, but
Dunn and Ravitz would be right along with him. Kilkenny
believed he could beat Cub, but he was not fool enough to
believe he could take all three.

There was always the chance of catching them off balance, as
he had taken the Brockmans.

The Brockmans! He had forgotten Cain. The big man was
free now to hunt him down. Would he do so? Had Kilkenny
sensed a growing respect in the man? Cain was a loner who did
not wish to ride alone. There had always been Abel before.
Now there was no one.

The big man was alone, and although big he might be, he
could move like a cat.

It was a three-cornered game now, and he had two to fear.
Two men who had committed themselves to killing him. Two
men who might appear at any time.

EIGHTEEN

As they worked their way back by a longer route, Kilkenny suddenly became worried. They had been gone a very long time, and the people at the Cup were few. Winding around, they climbed a steep mountainside, rode through a grassy bottom, and were entering the edge of the forest when far ahead of them they heard a rifle shot.

Instantly he clapped the spurs to his mount and went ghosting through the trees. The others, as if on command, spread out in a long skirmish line, each finding his own way through the forest.

Before him the Cup suddenly opened wide, and then he was coming down a little-used trail. He heard another shot and then saw a bunch of men scrambling for their horses. He slid to the ground and dropped to one knee. He fired as his knee touched the ground, and he saw one rider grab for the saddle horn, his shirt suddenly blossoming with crimson.

He fired three rapidly spaced shots, and down the line he heard others opening up as well. Then he was in the saddle and racing up to the house.

Jack Moffit lay sprawled on the ground, the rifle near his hand.

Sally ran from the house to him, and Ma Hatfield came out. "Hit us 'bout an hour back, maybe less. Jack, he'd been taking care of the stock when we heard them coming. Jack got off a shot and then run for the house. They nailed him before he made more'n three or four steps. I cut loose at them, and they holed up right quick. Bart, he rode in about that time and joined us. They nicked him, too."

Kilkenny dropped to his knees beside Jack. The boy had been grazed along the scalp, but the bad one was through his chest, high up.

Price Dixon dropped down beside him. Kneeling over the

143

boy, he conducted a swift, professional examination. "We'll have to get him inside on a table. That bullet has to come out."

Parson spat. "Ain't nobody here good enough to do that," he remarked, "although Ma's had a sight of experience."

"I'll do it," Dixon said. "I was a doctor once. Maybe I still am."

When they had the boy inside, Kilkenny went to the door with Parson. "This changes everything, Parson. I'd better go back in and get Nita. She won't be safe there now. This is wide-open war, and it has Cub's mark on it."

"You'd better take help. There's enough of us now to hold this place."

"I'll go alone. It is better that way, and I can move quieter and don't have to worry about where anyone else is."

"Don't you go to forgettin' Cain Brockman."

He glanced at Dixon. The man had taken a small, compact kit of tools from his saddlebags.

Parson jerked his head in Dixon's direction. "Says he's a doc. I hope he is."

"He is. I knew it the minute he went to work on my cut eye. I've seen professional handlers who were good, but not that good."

"You surely whupped Turner!" Hatfield said. "I d'clare, you surely did."

"I was lucky," Kilkenny said honestly. "I'm not as good a fighter as he is. It was simply that he wasn't expecting me to be as good as I was, and the fact that I had seen him fight before. If we fought again, Parson, he'd probably beat me."

"You whupped him."

"I whipped him today. I got him irritated there at the start, and he was too anxious to teach me a lesson, so I got in several good solid punches at the beginning before he was warmed up. Then he had the idea that I was just some husky cowhand, and he did not fight me as he would have a professional . . . and I've had professional training."

Kilkenny shook his head. "I'm no fool, Parson, and I know something of fighting. If we fought again, he'd beat me."

"You'd better get some rest, boy. That's a hard ride down an' back, and you've been through a lot. Let the doc there, if that's what he is, work over your face a mite, then you'd best catch some shut-eye. Won't do no good to go hightailin' it down there ready to drop out of the saddle. If the time comes when you face up to Cub Hale, you'd best be ready."

It made sense, and he took his blanket roll out under the trees again and stretched out. Until that moment he had not realized how thoroughly exhausted he was, but he had scarcely stretched out before he was asleep, and when he awakened, it was hours later and the sun was already down behind the mountains.

He rolled his bed and took it to his saddle. From long and grim experience he knew that whatever a man's plans might be, events can change them on the spur, and it paid to be ready. He never left a friend without the awareness that he might never see him again.

Price Dixon had operated, removing the bullet that endangered Jack Moffit's life. Constant manipulation of cards had at least kept his fingers deft and skillful, and from time to time in mining camps and elsewhere he had worked at his profession.

Kilkenny was not surprised to learn that he had been a skilled surgeon. The West was a haven for many kinds of people, and from all walks of life. Doctors, lawyers, judges, businessmen, European nobility, all thronged west looking for escape from what they had become or were becoming, or for adventure, quick wealth, whatever the West had to offer, and its promises and gifts were many.

Price Dixon and Lance Kilkenny had recognized each other from the first, not from any past experience together but as men from the same level, men of education and background, men of the lost legion of drifters, of whom there were many.

"The boy will live," Price told Kilkenny. "The bullet was dangerously near the spine, but it's out, and what he needs now is simply rest and plenty of good beef broth."

Sally Crane found him at the corral when he was saddling the gray horse he was riding that night. She came up in a great hurry and then suddenly stopped and stood silent, shifting her feet from place to place. Kilkenny glanced at her curiously from under the flat brim of his hat.

"What's the trouble, Sally?"

"I wanted to ask . . ." She hesitated shyly. "Do you think I'm old enough to marry?"

"To marry?" He straightened up, surprised. "Why, I don't know. How old are you, Sally?"

"I'm sixteen, nigh to seventeen."

"That's young," he conceded, "but I heard Ma Hatfield say she was just sixteen when she married, and in Kentucky and Virginia many a girl marries at that age. Why?"

"I reckon I want to marry," Sally said. "Ma Hatfield said I should ask you. Said you was Daddy Moffit's best friend and you was sort of my guardian."

"Me?" The idea startled him. "Well, I never thought of it that way, Sally. Who do you want to marry, Sally?"

"It's Bart. Mr. Bartram."

"Do you love him?" He suddenly felt strangely old, and looking at Sally, standing there so shy and yet so eager, he felt more than ever the vast loneliness that was in him, and also a tenderness such as he had never known before.

"Yes. Yes, I do."

"Well, Sally," he said, "I expect I am as much of a guardian as you have, and Moffit and I saw things pretty much alike. He would want the best for you, Sally, and if you love Bart and he loves you, I guess that's all that's needed, as he is a fine, straightforward sort of man. As soon as this trouble is cleared up, he will do all right. Yes, you can marry him."

She turned to start away.

"Sally?" She stopped, turning to face him. "Sally, remember one thing. Bart is a man who is going to grow. He will not stay the man he is, so if you marry him and want to be happy, you will have to grow with him.

"I've seen a lot of Bart, and he is a young man on his way. You can't just settle down and be blissfully happy and in love with him, because he is going to grow and he will be an important man in the community sometime. You will have to learn more and be more and be a credit to him."

"Oh, I will! I will!"

She was gone, running.

For a few moments he stood there, hands on the saddle, ready to mount. Then he stepped into the stirrup and threw his leg over the saddle. "Now, that is one thing you never expected to happen, Lance Kilkenny. Somebody asking you for permission to marry! Next thing I know, I'll have to give the bride away!"

He turned his horse into the trail. Men had died here. Men had built homes here. Now Sally and Bartram would be married. This was the country, and these were its people. They had the strength to live, to endure, to be. These were the people of simple tastes and simple virtues who were the backbone of the country, and not those vocal ones who were quick with words and prided themselves on their sophistication.

The little gray horse he was riding was as sure-footed as the buckskin. He spoke to it in a low whisper, and it flicked an ear to listen. This was a good horse, a steady, and quiet one.

He came up to Cedar in the darkness, with the stars about. He reined in, sensing something wrong, some change. The gray horse had its ears pricked, nostrils flaring. The smell of wood smoke was in the air, and a tension, an uneasiness. He looked down upon it, seeing only vague outlines, no lighted windows visible from where he sat. Something had changed, something was wrong.

He walked the gray horse forward, keeping to sandy or dusty places where it would make no sound. The black bulk of a building loomed before him, and the smell of smoke was stronger.

The Mecca was gone! Where Hale's place had stood was a heap of charred ruins.

What could have happened? An accident? No . . . it was something else, and behind the doors and windows he seemed to sense movement. The town only appeared to be asleep.

Keeping in the shadow of the barn, he moved forward. A faint light showed from Leathers' store, but the Crystal Palace was dark. Carefully keeping to the deepest shadow, he worked his way to the back of the Crystal Palace, leaving the gray under the trees near the abandoned building next door.

He had started out from the trees when a movement made him stop dead still.

A man was moving ahead of him, unaware of him, a huge man. He stopped, easing into the deeper shadow. It was Cain Brockman!

Watching, Kilkenny saw him moving with incredible stealth, saw him move to the door, work for a moment at the lock, then disappear inside.

Kilkenny crossed the intervening space in swift, soundless movement and went into the door after Brockman. Once inside, he flattened against the wall to present as small a target as possible for any possible shot.

He heard the big man ahead of him. On cat feet he moved after him.

What could Brockman want here? Was he after Nita? Or hoping to find him, to catch him off guard?

He moved along, closed a door behind him, lost Brockman in the still darkness. Suddenly a candle gleamed from an opening door. Nita was there in riding costume.

"You've come, Lance? It was you I heard?"

"It was not me," he said aloud, "it was Cain Brockman. He's here."

A shadow moved, and Cain Brockman said, "You bet I'm here."

Cain came back toward them, weaving among the card tables until he was scarcely fifteen feet away. The heavy drapes at all the windows were drawn, keeping all light within, but there was only the light of the candle. If he lived to be a thousand years old, Lance Kilkenny would never forget that room or that moment.

Brockman was there, huge, invulnerable, ominous.

It was a large room, and rectangular. Along one side was the bar; the rest of the room, except for the small dance floor across which they now faced each other, was littered with tables and chairs. There were the usual brass spittoons, fallen cards, scattered poker chips, cigarette butts, and glasses, all awaiting the cleanup man who would come at daybreak.

A balcony surrounded the room on three sides, a balcony with curtained booths.

Only the one tall, flickering candle. And Nita, her black hair gathered against the nape of her neck, her eyes unusually large in the dim light.

Facing him was Cain Brockman. His black hat was pushed back on his head, his thick neck descended into powerful shoulders, and a checkered shirt was open to expose a hairy chest. He wore crossed gun belts and his thumbs were tucked behind the belt within easy reach of the guns.

His flat face was oily and unshaved, his stance was wide, his feet in their boots seemed unusually small for such a large man.

"That's right," he said, "I'm here, Kilkenny."

Kilkenny drew a deep breath. A wave of something like hopelessness swept over him. He could kill this man. He knew it. Yet why kill him? Cain Brockman had come hunting him because it was the code of the life he lived and because the one anchor he had had been pulled loose, his brother, Abel.

At that moment Kilkenny saw Cain Brockman as he had never seen him before, a big, simple man, an earnest man who had drifted down the darker trails behind his brother. That one tie had been cut, and he stood here now, a lost man, with no destiny, no future. To kill Kilkenny was now his only purpose.

Kilkenny spoke calmly. "Cain, I'm not going to kill you. I'm not going to shoot it out with you. Cain, there's no sense in you and me shooting things up, no sense at all."

"What do you mean?" Brockman's brow furrowed. This was a puzzle. He knew Kilkenny too well to believe he was afraid.

"I don't want to kill you, Cain. You're too good a man. You and your brother teamed up with the wrong crowd down in Texas, and because of that we got into a shooting match. You looked for me, and I had to fight you. I didn't want to then, and I don't want to now.

"Cain, I owe something to those people in the mountains. I've a reason to fight for them. They are good, honest people and they are trying to build something. If I kill, it will be for that. If I die, I'd prefer it was in trying to keep their land for them. There's nothing to gain for either of us in a shoot-out. Suppose you kill me? What will you do then?"

Cain hesitated, puzzled. "Why, I'd go back to Texas."

"And then?"

"Go to ridin' for somebody, I guess."

"Maybe, Cain. And maybe some old acquaintance would come along and you'd rustle a few head or rob a stage. Then they'll get you like they did Sam Bass.

"You're a good man, Cain, and I'm not going to draw on you, and you're too good a man to shoot a man who won't fight. You've got too much good stuff in you to live the way you'll live and to die as you'll die, with a bullet or at the end of a rope."

Cain Brockman stared at him, and in the flickering candlelight Kilkenny waited. For the first time he was really afraid, afraid his words would fail and the big man would go for his gun. He honestly did not want to kill him, but his own instinct for self-preservation would make him draw if Cain did.

Suddenly Cain's hand went to his face, rubbing his grizzled chin. "Well, I'll be . . . I'll be eternally damned!"

He turned unsteadily and walked past Nita toward the door. He blundered into the doorjamb, then went out.

They heard his feet on the gravel, heard him pause, then walk slowly away into the night.

NINETEEN

Kilkenny stepped back and wiped the sweat from his brow. Nita crossed the room to him, her face radiant with relief.

"Oh, Lance! That was wonderful! Wonderful!"

"It was awful," he replied. "Just plain awful! I never want to go through that again."

He looked around. "Nita? Where is Brigo?"

"He's in my room, Lance. I was going to tell you when Brockman came. He's hurt, very badly."

"Brigo?" It seemed impossible. "How?"

"Two of Hale's gunmen, Dunn and Ravitz. Cub sent them after me. Brigo met them right here, and they shot it out. He killed both of them, but he was shot . . . three times."

"What's happened here, anyway? The Mecca has been burned."

"That was before Dunn and Ravitz came. Some miners were in the Mecca drinking. One of the miners had some words with a Hale gunman about your fight and about the nesters, and the miner proceeded to say what he thought about Hale.

"The gunman reached for his gun, and the miner hit him with a bottle, and that started it. Miners against the Hale riders. Oh, it was awful, Lance! It was bloody and terrible.

"Several of the Hale riders liked your fight and your attitude, and they quit. The miners outnumbered the others, and they drove them out of the Mecca, and in the process a lamp was knocked over and the place caught fire.

"Fighting continued in the street, but nobody used a gun. It was all rough-and-tumble, and by the time it was over, the Mecca had burned to the ground and the miners got into wagons and started back for Silver City or wherever they were from.

"For the next few hours it was like a morgue. Nobody was on the streets. They were littered with broken bottles, smashed chairs, and torn bunting. Everything was quiet then until Dunn and Ravitz came."

"Have you seen Cub?"

"No, but they say he's wild. He hated you and was furious when some of the men quit. He doesn't care about Halloran, for he's completely lawless. Also, he doesn't realize what Halloran can do to his father, or what all of this means. He cannot remember a time when his father was not a big man and able to do whatever he wanted.

"He's taken a dozen men and gone out after stolen cattle."

"Good! That means we have some time. Nita, you can't stay here. Ride to the Cup and send Price Dixon down here. If anybody can do anything for Brigo, he can. And you will be safe there."

"And you?"

"I'll be all right. Just send Dixon down here. Meanwhile, I'll get a buckboard and we'll be ready to take Brigo back with us."

They were silent, listening. There was no sound. The town had the silence of a grave.

"What about King Bill?"

"There are only rumors, Lance. Some of those cowhands who quit stopped in here for drinks. They said he acts like a man who's lost his mind. He was in here after the fight, but then he went to the Castle.

"He asked me to marry him, and I refused. He said he would take me anyway, and I told him Brigo would kill him if he tried. He went away, and it was then Cub sent those men after me.

"But something has happened to Hale. He's not the same man. He lost money to you, to the miners, and to Cain Brockman. He paid all his bets, even those for which he had not put up money. I don't believe the money mattered, but the losing did. He's never lost, he's never been thwarted, and he doesn't know how to cope with adversity. He was never a strong man insofar as character is concerned, and suddenly he has just seemed to come apart.

"We heard that Halloran told him the law would have to decide the nesters' case, and that if he had ordered Moffit and Miller killed, he would hang.

"Well, that was when he started to come apart. He had ruled like a little king here and had come to believe that he was almost that, and everything had gone about as he wanted until you came along."

"You mean everything went all right until he tried to turn some people out of their homes."

"Your whipping Turner really began it for him, for he did not actually hear of what happened in Blazer until afterward. I mean, he heard you tell Halloran about the nesters who were killed but I don't believe he realized he had lost men, too. Soderman in particular."

"What was that about stolen cattle?"

"When they left, some of his own hands drove off a herd he had planned to drive to Montana for the mining camps. Cub went after them."

"You must go," he urged. "Take my little gray. He's right out there under the trees. Don't worry about him. He can run all the way and not be breathing hard at the end."

She kissed him lightly on the lips and then was gone. He walked to the door to see her get into the saddle, and then turned back.

All was dark and still. The big Yaqui was asleep. He was breathing deeply and his face was flushed. Kilkenny laid a hand on his brow and it was hot, but he was sleeping and better left undisturbed.

Kilkenny walked back to the candle and checked his guns. Then he reloaded Brigo's guns and retrieved the shotgun kept under the bar. He found two more pistols, and both were loaded. He placed one on the bar and tucked the other in his waistband. Then he doused the candle and sat down in a chair from which he could watch both doors and hear Brigo's breathing.

It would be a long time until morning.

Twice during the long hours until daybreak he arose and paced restlessly about the great room or peered out into the ghostly street. Once something struck the broken glass of a bottle and he was out of his chair in an instant, but it proved to be only a lonely burro wandering along the dead street.

Toward morning he slept a little in snatches, every sense alert for trouble or for some stirring on the part of the big Yaqui.

Not until it was growing gray in the street and he had looked in on Brigo again did he think of food. He went into the big, empty kitchen and looked about, but found very little. He put on water for coffee, but the eating of the past weekend and the celebration had almost stripped the kitchen.

He went back to Brigo and found the big Yaqui awake. The Yaqui turned his head to look at him and Kilkenny said, "Nita

went to the Cup. She's sending Price Dixon down for you."
Then he added, "Turns out he's a doctor."

"I know. I know for long time about this."

"How do you feel?"

"Not good." Brigo was still, then he said, "Ver' weak."

"All right. You sit tight." He took the gun from the bar. "I'll
leave you with this. I'm going over to the store for grub. Be
right back."

The street was empty. He stepped out onto the porch and
closed the door behind him. There was no sound, not even a
squeaky pump or braying mule. He walked along the boardwalk to Leathers' store. He rattled the knob, and there was no
response. Without further hesitation he put his shoulder to the
door, lifted up on the knob, and pushed. The lock burst and
the door swung inward.

Leathers appeared from the back of the store. "Here!" he
exclaimed angrily. "What are you doing?"

"When I rattled the door, you should have opened it. I
figured maybe you wanted me to come right on in."

"That door was locked!"

"Was it, now?" He glanced innocently at the door. "Well,
what d' you know? It surely isn't locked now!"

"I told you once I wouldn't sell to you," Leathers protested.

"So you did," Kilkenny said mildly. "I figured you'd probably changed your mind. Where've you been the past few days,
Leathers? There's been some changes, and there will be more."

He threw a slab of bacon on the counter, put a dozen eggs
into a paper sack, and gathered a few other things he liked. He
kept the eggs separate but filled a burlap sack with other things
he thought might be needed, including two boxes of .44's.

From his pocket he took some money and dropped it on the
counter.

"Leathers," he said, "you're both a damn fool and a yellow-
belly. Why did you ever come west in the first place? This isn't
your kind of country. You're built for a small, very civilized
little community where you can knuckle under to authority and
crawl every time somebody looks at you. We don't much care
for that in the West, and they probably didn't like it wherever
you came from."

"Hale will get you for this!" Leathers said angrily.

"Leathers," Kilkenny said patiently, "hasn't it dawned on
you that Hale is finished? Half his men have quit, and some of
them are stealing his cattle. Hale himself has found a hole and

crawled into it. If he is still alive thirty days from now, he will be indicted for murder.

"You've spent your life living in the shadow of bigger men. Part of it is due to that sanctimonious wife of yours. If King Bill happened to smile at her, she'd walk in a daze for hours. The trouble is that she's a snob and you're a weakling.

"Take a tip from me. Take what cash you've got, enough supplies for the trip, and get out."

"And leave my store?"

"Within the next few hours Cub Hale will be riding into town with his outfit. They will be mad, and you know how much respect he has for you or anyone like you. If they don't clean you out, the Hatfields will.

"You refused supplies when we needed them, but now Hale is finished, and so are you. There's no place for you here any longer. If Cedar lasts, and I don't believe it will, we'll start from the ground up and build a new town, and we want men who will stand on their own two feet, like Perkins over in Blazer."

He walked back to the saloon and stored his grub.

Brigo was awake and had propped himself up a little. He had the gun in his hand.

Kilkenny went back to the kitchen, made coffee and some hot broth, which he took to Brigo. The big man was weak, so he fed him himself.

From time to time he went from window to window looking out. The sunlit street remained empty. Not a creature stirred. Yet the Hale riders would be coming back, and he wanted to get out before they did. From the back of the saloon he saw a buckboard standing at the side of a corral about fifty yards away.

Were there horses in the stable? Whose were they?

He scrambled some eggs, fried some bacon, and drank several cups of coffee.

Brigo had fallen asleep. He was flushed and feverish. The street was still empty, so Kilkenny went along the back of the buildings to the corral. There were several horses in the stable, so he harnessed two and led them out, leaving a note behind that the horses had been borrowed for an injured man and would be returned.

He hitched the horses to the buckboard and took it back to the Palace. From the back door he carried a mattress and some bedding and arranged them in the back of the buckboard.

He took the team to the usual place under the trees and tied them there, then went back to the saloon. Brigo was asleep, and he hesitated to awaken him, for sleep was the greatest curative, given the constitution Brigo had. He needed medical attention, and Doc Pollard, Hale's man, had fled to the Castle.

He went to the front door and barred it, then sat down at a table from which he could watch the street and waited.

He took up a spare deck of cards and riffled them in his fingers.

Nita was at the Hatfields' by now. At least he hoped she was. He had been a fool about her. He should have asked her to marry him before he left Texas. She would have come with him, and after all, he was not nearly so well known as Hardin or Hickok. He could just drop from sight.

Why not now? No use worrying about what he should have done, for the chance was here, now, staring him in the face. Suppose he did get killed eventually? Doesn't everybody die sometime? He had known for a long time that she was the girl for him, and lovely as the place in the high peaks was, he knew he could find another. Why not California? They did not know him there.

She was lovely to look at, tender and thoughtful, and above all, she was strong. She knew herself and what sort of person she was and wished to become.

Yet always the memory returned of the faces of the wives of other gunfighters, some of the fine men who had died bringing the law to little frontier communities. He had taken the news to more than one, and the bodies of their husbands to at least two. That was what had stopped him until now.

Bartram had Sally Crane. Soon they would be married. He remembered her sweet, youthful face, flushed with happiness. It made him feel old and tired.

The big Yaqui was still asleep. He tiptoed to the door and looked out. All was quiet. The clouds were building up around the peaks. If it rained, it would make it tough to move Jaime Brigo. Thunder rumbled like a whimper of far-off trumpets. He walked back to the table and sat down. Finally he went to the kitchen and got an apple from the stuff from Leathers' store.

He bit into it, and the sound was loud in the empty room.

TWENTY

They came down the dusty street through the sunlit afternoon, a tight little cavalcade of riders expecting no trouble. They rode as tired men ride, lounging in their saddles, for there was dust on their horses and dust on their clothing and dust on their beards. It was only their guns that had no dust.

There was no humor in them, for they were men to whom killing was a natural business. The softer members of the Hale crew were gone. These were the salty pick of a hard-bitten, lawless bunch who rode for the highest bidder.

Lee Wright was in the lead, riding a blood bay. At his right and a little behind was Jeff Nebel, then Tandy Wade, who was wanted in Texas, Missouri, and the Indian Territory, and then there was Kurt Wilde. They were ten in all, ten tough, gun-belted men riding into Cedar when the sun was high.

Dunn and Ravitz had not returned to the Castle, and what that meant they did not know, nor did they care. They had been sent to get a woman, and if Dunn and Ravitz had decided to keep her for themselves, they would take her away. If those two had failed and Brigo remained, they would take her from him. They had their orders and they knew what to do.

Near Leathers' store the group broke and three men rode on down to the Palace and dismounted at the door. Lee Wright, big, hard-faced, and cruel, was in the lead. With him were Wade and Wilde.

Kilkenny had seen them come, and he waited. As they stepped up on the walk, he took down the bar and opened the door. It was safer with the door closed, but he wanted to cut the odds down at the start, and he needed shooting room.

"What d' you want, Wright?"

"Who is it?" The shadows under the awning and the darkness of the doorway blurred his vision after the bright sunlight of the street.

"It's Kilkenny."

"Kilkenny! I don't believe it. Where'd you come from?"

"Been here all the time, Wright. Only, they call me Trent."

"Well, I'll be damned! Well, you got a chance to ride out of here with your reputation intact, Kilkenny. We just want that woman."

"But she's my woman, Wright," Kilkenny said softly. The three were spreading out a little. He had seen it so often before. "That makes a difference, doesn't it?"

They were wary. They had a job to do, but he was not part of it unless he made it so, but apparently he was doing just that. Yet they were tough men, worried less about him and his reputation than about who else might also be here. Nobody likes to walk into a stacked deck, and Brigo should be around somewhere. Also, if Kilkenny was here, there might be others.

Their lack of knowledge was half his strength.

"We were expecting you," he said. He was standing back from the doorframe, quite in the dark interior. He could see them, but they could see nothing of him, at best a dim outline. "I was wanting to tell you boys that I'd light a shuck, if I were you. The Hales are finished here."

"Do tell?" Wright was straining his eyes to see. "We come after that woman. We'll get her."

"Sorry, boys, but she's not even here. She's been gone for hours. As for taking her, you'd come after her with only ten men? Ever try to take a place like this with no more men than you've got?

"Anyway, who is going to pay you? I won most of Hale's money. By the time he paid off the miners, he was broke. You boys are working for nothing."

"We'll see about that."

"Don't try it, boys. The Hatfields like to use those rifles of theirs, and you fellows are sitting ducks out there in the bright light."

"You're runnin' a bluff!" Wade said. "You're alone."

"Where are they, then? You—"

There was a tinkle of glass from a window, and a rifle muzzle showed itself. Wright turned to look, and Kilkenny saw him swear soundlessly.

It could mean but one thing. Brigo had gotten out of bed and thrust a rifle out the window at the right moment. But how long could he stand there?

"Why fight for nothing? You try to take this place, and some of you will die and the rest won't get any payoff."

Kurt Wilde had been sitting quietly. Now suddenly he exploded with impatience. "The hell with this! Let's go in there!" He jumped his horse to one side and went for his gun.

Kilkenny palmed his gun and fired, the first shot clipping the bridle on the rearing horse, the second taking Wilde through the shoulder and knocking him into the street.

Brigo fired at almost the same instant, and Tandy Wade's horse caught the bullet meant for him and went down. Wade leaped free, and he and Wright sprinted for shelter.

Kilkenny slammed the door and dropped the bar in place and then sprinted for Brigo. The Yaqui's face was deathly pale, and the movement had started his wounds bleeding again.

"Lie down, dammit!" Kilkenny said. "You did your part. You fooled 'em. Now, lie down!"

"No, señor. Not when you fight."

"I can hold 'em now. Rest until I need you. If they rush the place, I'll need help."

Brigo hesitated, then let himself be taken back to the bed. He sank weakly down, and Kilkenny lifted his feet up. From where he lay he could see through a crack of the window without moving. Kilkenny dropped a rifle and a box of shells on the bed. Then he went back and made a round of the windows, peering from each.

Wilde was getting up. Kilkenny watched him, letting him go. Suddenly the man wheeled and blasted at the door. Brigo, lying on his bed, shot him through the chest.

"One down," Kilkenny told himself, "and nine to go!"

He had no illusions. These men were too old at the business to be fooled for long. Sooner or later they would rush the place, making a feint from one direction and charging from another. They had men enough, and he had too large an area to defend and there was no way he could watch it all. They could even come over the roofs and swing into the upper windows.

Kilkenny was looking toward Leathers' store when he saw a man slip around the corner of the building and dart for the door. He fired quickly. Once . . . twice.

The first shot hit the man about waist-high, but on the outside, near his holster. He staggered, and Kilkenny's second shot brought him down.

Kilkenny stood up and moved away just as a rifle bullet

struck right where he had been an instant before. Had he remained in position, he would now be dead or dying.

No chance to get Brigo to the buckboard. Not by daylight and probably not by night.

They came with a rush, finally.

It had been quiet, and then a sudden volley blasted the back of the saloon. Taking a chance, Kilkenny ran to the front and was just in time to see a half-dozen men charging the front of the Palace.

His first shot was dead center and knocked a Hale man rolling. His guns were roaring then, and he smelled the hot, acrid fumes of gunpowder, felt a red-hot whip laid across his cheek as a bullet grazed him.

He thrust a gun into its holster empty and drew the spare from his waistband.

They disappeared then, and he saw that two men were down. He recognized neither of them. He thrust the gun back into his waistband, and drawing the empty gun, fed shells into the loading gate. Then he checked his second gun, from which two rounds had been fired.

His cheek was burning like fire, and when he touched it, his hand came away bloody. He wiped the hand on a curtain and brought the shotgun up to the door, stuffing his pocket full of shells.

He waited. It was hot, and the waiting was what got to a man. He did not want to wait. He wanted to go get them. Three, possibly four of their men had been hurt or killed.

There was no firing now. Obviously they were doing some hard thinking. The shotgun was his payoff weapon, and knowing what it would do to a man at close range, he hesitated to use it.

He could hear voices raised in argument from Leathers' store. With three men hit and possibly four, they were undoubtedly having second thoughts. Suddenly he had an idea.

"Lie still and watch," Kilkenny said suddenly. "I'm going out."

"Out? You going after them?"

"Sí . . . with this." He showed him the double-barreled shotgun. "They are all in the store. I'm going to settle this, once and for all."

He went to the door. For several minutes he studied what lay outside and listened to the violent argument next door. Price Dixon would be arriving soon, and the Hale men undoubtedly knew he had joined Kilkenny and the Hatfields. He would be riding right into a trap from which there was no possible escape, unless he, Kilkenny, sprang the trap first. If Jaime Brigo was to live, he needed Dixon's attention, so both men's lives were at stake.

Kilkenny waited. The sun was making a shadow under the awning. He eased outside, then left the door with a quick soundless rush that took him to the wall of Leathers' store.

From here it was four good steps to the door, but there was no window to pass. He stepped up on the porch, knowing that if they had a man across the street he was a gone gosling.

He took a step and waited. He could hear Wright's voice inside. "Cub will pay off, all right. If he doesn't, we'll just take some cows."

"To hell with that! I don't want cows, I want money! An' I want out of this with a whole skin so's I can spend it."

"Pussonally," somebody drawled, "I don't see any sense in gettin' killed because somebody else wants a woman. I'll admit this Riordan gal is something to look at, but if she wanted a Hale she'd take one. I think she's crazy for Kilkenny, and for my money he's the best of the lot."

"What's it to you, Tandy?" Wright demanded. "Hale pays us. Besides, that Kilkenny just figures he's too damned good."

Tandy laughed. "Lee, I reckon if you want to prove you're better and ask him for a personal duel, he'll give it to you."

"Say!" Wright jumped to his feet. "That's it! That's the way we'll get him. I'll challenge him; then, when he comes into the street, we'll pour it into him."

There was a moment of silence. Kilkenny was just outside the door now. "Lee," Tandy said, "that's a polecat's idea. I'd have no part of such as that, an' you know it. I'm a fightin' man, not a murderer!"

"Tandy Wade," Wright warned, "someday you'll—"

"Suppose I take it from here?" Kilkenny interrupted.

He stood in the open door with his shotgun in his hands. Wright turned, his mouth open, his face suddenly discolored and ugly. Tandy Wade held his hands wide. He looked at the double-barreled shotgun and said, "Kilkenny, I guess that shotgun calls my hand."

"Buckshot in it, too," Kilkenny said casually. "I might be able to get more'n four or five of you gents at the one time, because she scatters pretty good at this range. I'd hate like the devil to blow you boys apart, but if you ask for it, what can I do?"

"Now, take it easy!" Wright protested. "I—"

"Leathers," Kilkenny said, "you just walk over here and collect their guns. Slap their shirts, too. I wouldn't want one of you boys to have a hideout gun and get your friends all shot up."

The storekeeper, shaking with fright, did as he was told, and no one said a word. These men were all too familiar with guns, and most of them had seen what a shotgun could do at that distance. When the guns were all collected and laid at his feet, he stood there for a moment looking at them.

"Wright, I heard you wanting to trick me and kill me."

Wright's expression was haunted and sick. "I talked too much. I wouldn't have done that."

There was a rattle of horses' hooves in the street, and Kilkenny saw hope flicker in Wright's eyes. "Careful, Lee!" Kilkenny spoke quietly. "If I go, you go with me."

"I ain't movin'! For God's sake, don't shoot!"

TWENTY-ONE

Now the horses slowed to a walk, and they drew up before the Crystal Palace. Kilkenny dared not turn. He dared not look. Putting a toe behind the stack of guns, he pushed them back, then farther back. Then he waited. A slight turn of his head, and they would rush him en masse; he might get off a shot, and might not. Certainly he would be dead within the minute.

Sweat beaded his forehead, and his mouth was utterly dry. He tried to swallow and could not. They had just to walk up behind him. He backed to one side of the door, but kept his eyes on them. Even for an instant he dared not avert his eyes. His only way was to go out fighting.

Looking into the eyes of the men before him, he could see what was in their minds. Their faces were gray and sick. A shotgun wasn't an easy way to die, and once that gun started blasting, there was no telling who would be hit. And Kilkenny with an empty shotgun still had two guns on his hips and one in his waistband. And every man there had heard what Kilkenny could do with a six-gun.

The flesh was crawling on the back of Kilkenny's neck and he saw Wright's tongue feeling for his dry lips. Only Tandy Wade seemed relaxed. The tension showed only in his eyes. They could hear boots now, coming along the boardwalk, and more than one pair. Two men walking.

At any moment now this room could turn into a section of bloody hell. A door slammed at the Crystal Palace.

Had Brigo passed out? Was he dead? There was no sound of walking now, but they all knew somebody was crossing the dusty space between the boardwalks that fronted the two buildings. Suddenly the boots were close. Only five steps . . .

Leathers slipped to the floor in a dead faint. Tandy looked down at him with contempt.

If that was Cub Hale behind him, he would be killed, but he would go out taking a bloody dozen with him, and he would not drop his gun if ordered. He would simply open fire.

He clicked back the hammers.

"No! For God's sake, Kilkenny!" He did not know who spoke.

These men who could face a shoot-out with composure were frightened and pale at the gaping mouth of the shotgun.

"Kilkenny?" The voice was behind him, and it was Parson Hatfield's voice.

"Come in, Parson. I reckon everybody's glad to see you."

Tandy Wade struck a match and lit the cold cigarette in his lips. "I can't speak for the others," he said, "but, Parson, you're about the best-appearing man I ever did see, an' you did your best appearing just now!"

Hatfield came in, and Bartram and Runyon were with him. "Where's Cub Hale?" Parson demanded.

"He cut off for the Castle. He figured Dunn and Ravitz would have the girl there," Wade volunteered. "When she wasn't there, he sent us after her."

"He must have stopped off on the way, because he wasn't there. The place was deserted, not a soul around until we went inside the house. Hale was there. He'd shot himself."

"I think he saw us coming," Runyon said. "I heard a shot."

"What happens to us?" Tandy Wade asked.

Before he could speak, Parson Hatfield interrupted. "We want Jeff Nebel and Lee Wright. Both of them were in on the killin' of Moffit, and both were there when Miller was killed, and Nebel hisself killed Smithers. Least, that's the way we hear it."

"Take them, then," Kilkenny said. His eyes went to Wade. "I heard what you said when I was outside the door. You're too good a man to run with this crowd, Tandy. You ride out of here before you wind up at the end of a rope."

"Thanks, man," Wade said. "It's more than I have coming."

"You others, get on your horses and get out of here, just leave, and if you ever show up in this country again, we'll hang you."

They scrambled for the door. Hatfield was already gone with Wright and Nebel.

Leathers was on his feet. He looked sick and empty. "You've got twenty-four hours," Kilkenny said. "Take what you can and get out. Don't come back."

He walked out of the store and into the dusty street. He wanted to see how Price was doing with Brigo, but two men on horseback were coming down the street riding together.

Dan Cooper and Cain Brockman. They rode right up to him. Cooper took out the makings and began to roll a smoke. "Looks like I backed the wrong horse," he said. "What's the deal? Got a rope for me? Or do I draw a ticket out of here?"

"What do you want?"

"Well, me an' Cain here been talkin' some. We both won money on your fight and we both like high mountain country, so we thought if you'd have us we'd like to file on some of that mountain country."

"Right pretty places up there," Cain said, waiting. "If you say so, we'll drift."

Kilkenny looked from one to the other, then said, "Be pleased to have you. Cain, that Moffit place is empty now. Jack won't be able to handle a place like that, so if you want to make a deal for it, or work it on shares, you could start off with a ready-built house.

"Dan, the Smithers place is empty. We might work something out with his family. Otherwise, there's still some good land open up there. Be glad to have you."

He went next door to the Palace, and as he walked in, Nita came over to him. "He's going to be all right, I think," she said. "Price fixed him up as best he could, and he's with him now."

"Good." Kilkenny took her in his arms. He drew her close, and her lips melted into his, and for a long time they stood holding each other.

"Oh, Lance!" she whispered. "Don't let me go. Keep me now. It has been so long, and I've been so lonely."

"Yes, I'll keep you now, Nita. I have been lonely, too. We'll just have to chance what the future holds. It is better to be together."

Slowly, in the days that followed, the country came back to itself. Widows of two of the nesters moved into Leathers' house and took over the store. Kilkenny and Bartram helped them get organized and in business. The ruins of the Mecca were cleared away. Van Hawkins, a former actor from San Francisco, came in and bought the Crystal Palace from Nita, and Kilkenny began building a newer and more comfortable house on the site of the old one. Yet through it all there was much uneasiness. Kilkenny talked much with Nita in the evenings, and he saw the dark circles under her eyes. She was sleeping very little, he knew. And he knew why.

The Hatfields went nowhere without arms, and Steve Runyon, who before the trouble had rarely carried a gun, now carried one wherever he went. No one ever mentioned Cub Hale, but he was on everyone's mind. He had vanished mysteriously after the suicide of his father, leaving no trace. There was no hint of what he planned or what he was to become.

Then one day Saul Hatfield rode up to Kilkenny's claim and stopped by to watch the work on the house. He leaned on the saddle horn and looked down at Lance.

"How's things? Seems you're doin' right well with the house."

"It's going up. How's your father?"

"Pert. Right pert. Pa, he never changes very much. Complains a mite when cold weather comes. Got hisself rheumatism, I guess."

"They digging those potatoes of Smithers'?"

"I reckon. He had him a good crop."

"He'd like that. He was a thrifty man." Lance put a hand on the horse. "What's on your mind, Saul?"

"Quince an' me was down on the branch. Seen some horse tracks there . . . fresh ones. Somebody had crossed the stream and gone down into the rough country. Well, we follered them tracks. Found some white hairs on the bark of a tree."

Cub Hale had always ridden a white horse. An albino, it was.

"Which way was he heading?"

"He was going down into the wilderness country we crossed to go to Blazer. Now, there's no reason for a man to ride into that country unless he has to, although it might be a good place for a hideout. Nobody likely to come upon him yonder."

"Did you back-trail him?"

"Uh-huh. Seemed to have circled around Cedar like he was lookin' the place over."

"I reckon I'd better ride down to Cedar, Saul. I been needing a few things, anyway, and I might stick around a few days."

"Sho." Saul straightened up. "A body could foller them tracks. It was a plain trail."

"Dangerous. Like trackin' a grizzly."

Kilkenny saddled the long-legged yellow horse with the black legs and started for town. Cub Hale wasn't going to pull out until he had done some meanness, as Saul would have said, and he was a man who was driven to kill, even if he died in the process. Lance had never believed Cub would leave. The younger Hale had been holed up somewhere, licking his mental wounds and building hatred.

Kilkenny rode right to the cottage where Nita was living. Sally was staying with her, and Nita was helping the younger girl get ready for her wedding.

Nita came to the door with her sewing in her hand. She saw by his face that something was wrong. "Lance? Is it Cub?"

"He's around, Nita. Looks like you've got a guest for dinner."

"Put your horse in the barn and come on in. There's oats in the bin."

"Spoil a good horse," he grumbled. "That buckskin will be heading over here every time I get on him."

"That's the idea," she said cheerfully. "Just so you come with him, I'm going to feed you, too."

He was seated by the window when he saw Quince and Saul ride in, and a few minutes later Dan Cooper and Cain Brockman.

Brockman went to the Palace and apparently had a drink, then came out and began to loaf on the porch. There was a bench there, and he sat down and lit a cigar.

Kilkenny swore softly to himself. Nita looked up. "What's the matter?"

"That lot . . . they think I need protection."

"Good for them. How do you know if Cub will be alone?"

Well, he didn't, and he might not be. There were always drifting hard cases willing to tie up with anybody who could lead them into money or trouble.

The room was very pleasant. There were lace curtains at the windows, some china plates on shelves, and a few pictures on the walls. Nita dried her hands on her apron and called them to lunch. He took a quick look along the street, then went to the table. Sally's face was very flushed and pretty.

Bartram knocked and then entered. Kilkenny grinned at Sally. "No wonder you were looking so excited."

"It's not often a man gets to try his wife's biscuits before he marries her," Bart said, "but these are sure good!"

"Tell Nita, then, and not me. She's the one who made them."

"Nita? I didn't even know you could cook."

"That's not true, Lance. I've cooked for you before."

The door opened, and Cain Brockman loomed in the opening. "Kilkenny? Shall I take him? He's riding in."

"No." Kilkenny touched his lips with the napkin. "If he wants trouble, it's me he wants."

His eyes met Nita's across the table. "Don't pour my coffee. I like it hot."

He walked to the door. Far down the street he could see Cub Hale on his white horse. As he watched him, Cub rode to the rail, dismounted, tied his horse, and hung his hat on the pommel. Then he started up the middle of the street.

Kilkenny went outside and stepped down off the porch. The roses around the steps were in bloom, and their scent was strong in his nostrils. He could smell the rich, fresh-turned earth in the garden patch, and somewhere a magpie screeched.

He opened the gate and stepped out, closing it carefully behind him.

It was best to have this over now, to have it behind him rather than letting it become a nightmare of waiting. He did not want it, but here it was.

Saul Hatfield was standing on the steps of the store, his rifle in the hollow of his arm. Cain was tilted back in a chair in front of the store. The other men who had been sitting on the bench near him had vanished. Quince was sitting in front of an old adobe with his rifle across his knees. Just in case he failed.

Failed? He had never failed. Yet sooner or later everyone did. There was always the time when they started a mite too slow, the gun hung in the holster, or a cartridge misfired.

The air was hot, but in the distance thunder rumbled. Soon it would be raining on their crops. That was another thing. They got more rain up there than down here. A few scattered drops fell. Odd, he had not even noticed it was clouding up. One of those quick, hard mountain thunderstorms, he supposed.

He could see Cub more clearly now. Always freshly shaved when Lance had seen him on other occasions, he was unshaved now. He was not wearing his fancy buckskin jacket. Only the guns were the same, and the eyes that seemed to burn.

Abruptly Hale stopped, and when he stopped, Kilkenny stopped too. He stood there, perfectly relaxed, waiting. Cub's face was white and pasty. Only his eyes seemed alive.

"I'm going to kill you!" His voice was sharp and strained.

"You needn't, you know. You can always ride out of here and forget it."

The words were empty, and he knew there could be no words now. Somebody had to die. Yet it was all wrong. He felt no tension, no alertness. He was just standing there, feeling a great pity. Why would they never learn that nothing was ever solved with a gun?

Something flickered in those strange eyes, and Kilkenny, standing perfectly erect, slapped the butt of his gun with his palm, and the gun leaped up, settling into a rocklike grip. The gun bucked in his hand, almost of its own volition. It bucked hard against his grip, twice.

The gun before him flowered with flame, and something white-hot struck him low down on his right side. The gun boomed again, but the bullet wasted itself in the dust, and Cub's knees buckled. There was a spot of growing crimson on his chest, right over the heart.

Cub Hale fell facedown in the dust, then straightened his legs, and there was silence in the long dusty street of Cedar.

Kilkenny stood perfectly still, thumbing shells into his gun to replace the empties. He holstered the gun and started back up the hill toward the cottage, but somehow it seemed unusually steep. He walked on, and he could see Nita opening the gate and running to him.

He stopped then, feeling something wet against his leg. He looked down, and there was blood on his side. He walked on, his legs feeling stiff and awkward, and Nita met him in the street.

"Lance? Oh, Lance . . ."

"I'm all right," he said.

Cain Brockman suddenly had an arm around his shoulders, and Quince was on the other side.

He was sitting in a chair when Price Dixon came in. "If you fellows keep on shooting, I'll just have to hang up my shingle," he said.

"He's all right," he said later. "The bullet hit him atop the hipbone. Flesh wound and some shock. He'll be all right."

Later, Nita came in. "Shall I pour your coffee now?" she asked lightly.

"Let Sally pour it," he said. "You stay here."